So B. It

A NOVEL

BY SARAH WEEKS

LAURA GERINGER BOOKS

HarperTrophy®

An Imprint of HarperCollins*Publishers*

To David—
who's taught me so much about both
knowing and not knowing.
With love
—S.W.

So B. It

Copyright © 2004 by Sarah Weeks

All rights reserved. No part of this book may be used or reproduced
in any manner whatsoever without written
permission except in the case of brief quotations embodied in crit-
ical articles and reviews. Printed in the United States of America.
For information address HarperCollins Children's Books, a divi-
sion of HarperCollins Publishers, 1350 Avenue of the Americas,
New York, NY 10019.
www.harperchildrens.com

Library of Congress Cataloging-in-Publication Data
Weeks, Sarah.
So B. It : a novel / by Sarah Weeks.—1st ed.
    p.   cm.
Summary: After spending her life with her mentally retarded
mother and agoraphobic neighbor, twelve-year-old Heidi sets out
from Reno, Nevada, to New York to find out who she is.
ISBN-10: 0-06-441047-1
ISBN-13: 978-0-06-441047-2
[1. Identity—Fiction. 2. Mothers and daughters—Fiction. 3.
Mental illness—Fiction.]
PZ7.W42235 So 2004   2003015643
[Fic]—dc22   CIP
                                                            AC

Typography by Alicia Mikles
❖
First Harper Trophy edition, 2005

CONTENTS

CHAPTER ONE

Heidi

If truth was a crayon and it was up to me to put a wrapper around it and name its color, I know just what I would call it—*dinosaur skin*. I used to think, without really thinking about it, that I knew what color that was. But that was a long time ago, before I knew what I know now about both dinosaur skin and the truth.

The fact is, you can't tell squat about the color of an animal just from looking at its bones, so nobody knows for sure what color dinosaurs really were. For years I looked at pictures of them, trusting that whoever was in charge of coloring them in was doing it based on scientific fact, but the truth is they were only guessing. I realized that one afternoon, sitting in the front seat of Sheriff Roy Franklin's squad car, the fall before I turned thirteen.

Another thing I found out right around that same time is that *not knowing* something doesn't mean you're stupid. All it means is that there's still room left to wonder. For instance about dinosaurs—were they the same color as the sky the morning I set off for Liberty? Or were they maybe the same shade of brown as the dust my shoes kicked up on the driveway at Hilltop Home?

I'd be lying if I said that given a choice, I wouldn't rather know than not know. But there are some things you can just know for no good reason other than that you do, and then there are other things that no matter how badly you want to know them, you just can't.

The truth is, whether you know something or not doesn't change what was. If dinosaurs were blue, they were blue; if they were brown, they were brown whether anybody ever knows it for a fact or not.

CHAPTER TWO

Dette

One thing I knew for a fact, from the time I knew anything at all, was that I didn't have a father. What I had was Mama and Bernadette, and as far as I was concerned, that was plenty. Bernadette started off being the next-door neighbor, but that didn't last for very long. My mother loved me in her own special way, but she couldn't take care of me herself because of her bum brain. Bernie once explained it to me by comparing Mama to a broken machine.

"All the basic parts are there, Heidi, and from the outside she looks like she should work just fine, but inside there are lots of mysterious little pieces busted or bent or missing altogether, and without them her machine doesn't run quite right."

And it never would.

Bernadette understood about Mama. She knew how to talk to her and how to teach her things. The trick with Mama was to do things over and over the exact same way every single time until she got it. That's how Bernadette taught Mama to use the electric can opener. Every day for weeks she brought over the cat food cans and opened them in front of Mama.

"Watch me, Precious," she'd say. "Lift up. Put the can under. Press down. Listen to the hum. Done."

Pretty soon Mama was saying the words along with her. Well, not all of them, but she'd nod her head and say "Done" when that part came. After a while Bernadette let Mama try it herself. At first she couldn't remember what to do—she got the order all mixed up—but Bernie kept working with her and talking softly to her, and finally one day Mama opened a can all by herself.

"Done."

I don't know who was happier about it, Bernadette or Mama.

After that Mama opened cans all the time.

Soup and cat food and tuna fish. Any kind of can. In fact, we had to keep them hidden up high, or over at Bernadette's, because if Mama saw a can, she opened it, whether you happened to need what was inside it right then or not.

Bernadette's apartment was right next to ours, and in the olden days, when the building was first built, the rooms were probably all joined together as one big apartment. That's why there was a connecting door between us. That door meant that when Bernadette came over, she didn't actually have to leave her apartment, which was a lucky thing for Mama and me because of Bernadette's "A.P."

When she first explained it to me, I thought she said she had *angora phobia*. I looked it up in M.B.F. (Man's Best Friend), which is what we called the big Webster's dictionary we kept on the coffee table in the living room. It said a phobia was a fear and angora was a long-haired animal, usually a goat or a rabbit. I wasn't sure why, but when you put them together, according to Bernadette, it meant you were afraid to leave your house.

Later on I learned that what Bernie had was actually called *agora*phobia, not *angora* phobia, but it still boiled down to the same thing—she didn't go outside. Ever. She couldn't, because if she did, something terrible would happen. She never told me what exactly, but from the look she got in her eyes just thinking about it, I knew it was bad.

Bernadette loved to read. She always had her nose stuck in a book, and if not her nose then she'd have a finger in there, holding her place while she did whatever else needed doing quickly so she could get back to her reading.

"Did you know that an ostrich's eye is bigger than its brain, Heidi?"

She was always telling me interesting stuff that she'd found in some book. If she was reading about Africa, she wouldn't tell me something boring about irrigation ditches—she'd tell me, "Elephants are the only four-legged animals that can't jump."

Every night as far back as I can remember, Bernadette read out loud to me before I went to sleep. The two of us would tuck Mama in together, and then Bernie would come in and sit on my bed and read to me until I couldn't keep my eyes open anymore.

She read me *Charlotte's Web* and *The Little Prince*, parts of the Bible, and Zen philosophy. She translated *Romeo and Juliet* into English, well, my kind of English, and we both cried at the ending. She read me Greek myths and Nancy Drew mysteries, the biography of Mahatma Gandhi, and all the Little House books twice through. Bernadette and I couldn't go outside together, but every night we rode bareback across the prairie in calico bonnets or belly crept into dark caves or followed clues up steep winding staircases into the tops of mysterious clock towers.

Bernie taught me everything I knew, and she was a very good teacher. When she explained things, they shot into my brain like arrows and stuck. She could describe an Arctic blizzard or cross-pollination, and suddenly I'd be leaning into the bite of a freezing wind or riding a bumblebee's back right into the middle of a snapdragon. Nobody *ran* in Bernadette's world—they "skittered" or "high-tailed it." They didn't *whine*, they "puled and moaned." She knew a million words, and when she couldn't find one to fit, she'd make one up. Like when Mama got frustrated and started scrunching up her face and working her jaw, Bernadette would say:

"Your mama's cooking up a royal rimple, Heidi."

"A royal rimple" sounded like some kind of fancy pudding to me, but Mama cooked them up on a pretty regular basis, and believe me, hers didn't come with whipped cream and a cherry on top. Usually they happened when Bernadette was trying to teach her something new. Some things Mama could learn, like how to open cans, but there were some things that no matter how hard Bernadette tried, Mama just couldn't get. Like how to tie her shoes.

"Right over left. Snake in the tunnel. Pull tight. Make loops. Right over left. Snake in the tunnel. Pull tight. Done."

I must have heard Bernadette say that a million times. In fact, I still hear her voice in my head saying those very words every time I tie my own shoes, because that's the way she taught me. But Mama couldn't get it. After a few tries she started banging her head on the table shouting, "Done! Done! Done!" and she wouldn't stop until Bernadette finally bent down and tied her shoes for her.

Bernadette was not what you'd call a quitter, but she understood that some things were just too hard for Mama. That's why when she ordered shoes for her from a catalogue, she always got the slip-on kind.

I loved my mother, and I know she loved me too, but if we hadn't had Bernadette, we'd have been in big trouble. Mama didn't know things. She didn't understand numbers at all. She couldn't tell time or use money or the telephone. She only knew one color, blue, and although she could recognize a few letters, *A* and *S* and sometimes *H*, she couldn't read, not even her own name.

Bernadette taught me how to read and write when I was five. She said I took to it like a duck, which I remember thinking was a strange expression. I'd never heard of a duck that could read. But if Bernadette had told me there was such a duck, I would have believed her without hesitation. As far as I was concerned, she knew everything there was to know, but that was before I left Reno in search of a four-letter word and discovered along the way that people know only what they know and nothing more than that.

CHAPTER THREE

Hello

Mama never had a job and Bernadette didn't work either. I was the only one in my family who was ever employed. When I turned nine, I began to baby-sit twice a week for the Chudacoff twins, who lived on the sixth floor. Mrs. C gave violin lessons to the neighborhood kids, and I watched her kids for $2.50 an hour while she did it. I made ten bucks a week. It seemed like a lot of money at the time, but of course it was nowhere near enough for Mama and me to live on.

Every month like clockwork Bernie heard from the gas company, the electric company, the phone company, and the landlord, but Mama and I never got even one bill. We didn't have a phone, but we had a decent-size two-bedroom apartment with heat and electricity running through it just like everybody else; we just weren't paying for it.

"If Mama and I aren't paying, doesn't that mean we're stealing?" I asked Bernadette one day.

"Well, I guess some people might think so, but I think of it differently, Heidi. Some people fall through the cracks in life and end up living in cardboard boxes on the street. You and your mama just fell through a luckier set of cracks is all."

It was Bernadette who first discovered my lucky streak. We were playing a new game she'd ordered for me, called Memory. It's made up of little cardboard cards with pictures on them, which you mix up and turn facedown on the table. The idea is to take turns flipping over cards two by two trying to find matching pairs. It's supposed to test your memory by making you try to recall where you saw the kitty or the umbrella the last time, so you can turn over that same card again when you find the match for it later on somewhere else. For me, though, memory had nothing to do with it.

On my very first turn I flipped up the

center card. It was a yellow duck. Then for no particular reason, I decided to flip up the card in the upper left-hand corner. There was the other yellow duck.

"Lucky guess!" Bernadette said.

Only I did that same thing twenty more times in a row. Bernadette never even got a turn. Every guess I made was lucky. I never had to test my memory, because I found all the matches without missing once. It was easy. I didn't even have to think about it—just reached out and turned over card after card making perfect matches.

"How in the world did you do that, Heidi-Ho?" Bernadette asked, looking at the cards and stroking her chin.

I didn't know how I'd done it. But when she shuffled the cards and set them on the table facedown, I did it all over again.

"I'll be hornswoggled," Bernadette said.

I'm not psychic—I can't tell the future or see things that are happening somewhere else or talk to people who've died. I know, because after the lucky Memory games, Bernadette tested me on all that. I explained to her again and again that I didn't *see* the matches in my head, I *guessed* where they might be. It wasn't anything fancy like ESP; I was just plain lucky.

One place my luck came in very handy was at the Sudsy Duds Laundromat on the corner. There was a slot machine in the back near the bathrooms, and I had a real sweet way with it. Even though Bernadette hated to send me down there, I had to go to the Sudsy Duds fairly regularly. My baby-sitting money only went so far at the grocery store.

Bernadette wouldn't have hesitated to give me or Mama the last drop of water she had if we'd all been dying of thirst in the desert, but she didn't have any money to spare. Before Mama and I came to Reno, Bernie had lived in her apartment with her father, just the two of them. On the night of his seventy-fifth birthday they went out to a diner for supper. He ate a pot roast sandwich and two slices of yellow cake, and on the way home he dropped dead of a heart attack. I used to think that was something that made me and Bernadette alike, the fact that neither of us had a father, but there was a big difference. I didn't miss mine. I had never met him, I didn't know his name. I never even thought about him. But Bernadette missed her dad. It was right after he died that she came down with her A.P.

Bernie's dad left her some money. It wasn't much, but she kept it in the bank and called it her nest egg, and it was enough for her to get by on. When we needed extra cash for food or for something out of the ordinary, like a new part for the vacuum cleaner, my luck was the tin can we used to bail out our boat and keep us afloat.

"You know how I hate to send you down there, but as long as you don't abuse your gift, Heidi, or God forbid get caught, I don't believe it's a sin for you to play the slots," Bernie used to say whenever I went down to the Sudsy Duds. "Not so long as there's a good reason for it. The day I send you down there to try to charm enough change out of that machine to deck me out in a mink stole, that'll be the day I deserve to be struck by lightning, no questions asked."

I wasn't exactly sure what Bernadette meant by "abusing my gift," but I knew all about how not to get caught. It's illegal for a minor to gamble in Reno, but there were ways to get around that. I was always tall for my age, and since Bernie was pretty short, by the time I was ten, I was able to wear most of her clothes—even her shoes. A lot of Bernie's blouses and dresses were old and faded, with mismatched buttons and safety-pinned zippers. Hems were usually tacked up with staples because it was faster than needle and thread. I'd stand on a chair in whatever outfit we'd picked out for me, and Bernie would walk around me with the stapler, taking quick tucks here and there until things fit right.

My hair was thick and dark and impossibly curly. Sometimes it got so knotted, the only way to get a comb through it was to snip out the snarls with a nail clipper. I wished my hair could be straight like Bernie's. When hers was loose, she could tuck the ends under herself and actually sit on it. I tried to grow mine long like that too, but for some reason it never seemed to make it past my shoulder blades. Bernie combed and brushed my hair for me every morning and again each night before bed. She called it my wild mane, and we joked that she was the only one who was really able to tame it. When I needed to pay a visit to the Sudsy Duds, she would sit me down in a kitchen chair and give me "a do." She'd pull it back flat against my head, twist it, and pin it up into a hairdo she called a "cruller."

"Just like Tippi Hedren in *The Birds*," she told me.

With my hair up, wearing one of Bernie's dresses and a pair of pumps, all I needed was a touch of lipstick to complete the look.

"Fly under the radar, Heidi," Bernadette would say as she tied a filmy scarf over my hair to keep the wind from blowing it loose. "And remember, baby, *listen to the eyes*."

Bernie believed the only way to tell if a person could be trusted was to listen to what the eyes told you.

"People have all kinds of tricky ways to keep you from seeing who they really are, Heidi, but trust me, the eyes give them away every time," she'd say.

Bernie saw all kinds of things in people's eyes I never would have noticed. She made me practice by looking at pictures of faces in magazines. To me they always looked like perfectly nice people, but then Bernie would show me how I'd missed a certain mean glimmer or a hooded lid that should have tipped me off right away about the person's shady nature.

I always won when I went to the Sudsy Duds, enough to cover whatever we needed. I would bring home my winnings, and Bernie would run hot soapy water in the sink and wash all the money. She washed every bit of cash that came into the house—paper and coins both.

"You never know where it's been or who might have touched it along the way," she'd say.

I loved the way the green bills looked when she hung them over the shower rod to dry. When I brought home nickels, she would scrub them with the dish brush until they gleamed. Then she'd dump them out on a big towel on the kitchen table to dry, after which I would carefully turn them all heads up.

"It's good luck for them to match," I'd say.

"If you say so, Heidi-Ho. You're certainly the expert on luck around this house. Lord knows that lucky streak of yours explains a lot," Bernadette often said.

"What does it explain?" I'd ask.

"How you and your mama came to be standing outside my door way back when, that's what," she'd say.

"How did we?" I'd ask, even though I'd heard the story more times than I could count.

We don't know exactly when my birthday is because I don't have a birth certificate, and Mama didn't know when her own birthday was, let alone mine. So we celebrated on February twelfth because as close as she could figure, I was about a week old on February nineteenth, which is when Bernadette found Mama and me standing in the hallway outside her door.

The way she told it, she heard this pitiful sound and thought that one of her cats had gotten out somehow and couldn't get back in. She opened the door a crack and saw Mama standing there in her raincoat, her bare legs spattered with dried mud. And she saw me wrapped in a blanket, crying.

I don't remember it at all, of course, but I heard Bernadette tell the story so many times I feel as though I do. She said she never saw a sorrier sight in her life. She opened the door a little wider and Mama and I walked into her apartment and straight into her heart forever. That's how Bernie told it anyway.

Mama handed me to Bernie along with an empty baby bottle and a can of powdered formula, then she went and sat down in the big blue chair by the window, waiting there with her right arm kind of crooked and the left one resting in her lap, just as though she was holding an invisible baby.

I was not the sweetest-smelling child she'd ever run across, so Bernadette ran warm water in the kitchen sink and gave me a bath. She didn't have any diapers around, of course, so she fashioned one for me from a tea towel and a couple of pieces of duct tape. After she'd cleaned me up, she held me while she made my bottle, then took me to Mama and slipped me right into her perfectly positioned waiting arms. Mama fed me the bottle, which I sucked down in such a hurry, Bernadette thought I might choke. Then I fell sound asleep, at which point, without a word, Mama stood up and walked out, closing the door behind her.

Bernie watched through the peephole as Mama carried me down the hall into our apartment.

Bernie said she worried about us all day, but because of the A.P. she couldn't come knock on our door. It nearly killed her, knowing we were right next door and she couldn't get to us. Several times she opened her door a crack and called out, hoping Mama would hear her and open the door, but she didn't. So she paced around her apartment for hours trying to figure out what to do.

She thought about calling the police, but she was worried they might not know how to do right by Mama and me. Bernie didn't trust anyone from outside. She thought about trying to crawl down the hall to us on her stomach. But she knew she wouldn't make it. That's when she remembered the old door she'd once noticed at the back of her hall linen closet. She ran to the closet, unloaded the bottom two shelves, and yanked them out so she could get close enough to press her ear up against the door. She heard me crying on the other side!

There was no knob on the door, but it wasn't boarded up or nailed shut, so she got a screwdriver and stuck it in where the knob should have been. A couple of jiggles and the door popped open "like a jar of pickles." There I was, lying on a pillow in the middle of the kitchen floor still wearing that soggy tea towel, bawling with my little fists clenched tight as crab apples, Mama curled up in her raincoat next to me sound asleep.

From that day forward Bernadette came and went through the old door that connected our two apartments. She taught Mama how to warm my bottles and dip her elbow into the water to see if the temperature in the tub was just right. Whatever Bernadette couldn't teach Mama to do for me, she did for me herself. Read to me, sang to me. Taught me to read and write. Bernadette said she thought that I was born lucky, but I think the day she came through the connecting door and found Mama and me on the kitchen floor was probably the exact moment my good luck kicked in.

CHAPTER FOUR

Soof

When Bernadette first started coming to our apartment, she said, it was practically empty. There were a few pieces of mismatched furniture, some clothes hanging in the closets, odds and ends in the kitchen drawers and cupboards, a couple of baby things, a box of Jujyfruits, but not much else. She looked around for anything that might have a name on it, a letter or an address book, a purse or a wallet, but there was nothing. She said it was as though Mama and I had dropped out of the sky.

I'm not sure if Bernadette was a natural-born pack rat or if it was out of necessity that she never threw anything away. Until the time I was old enough to go downstairs to take out the trash, if something didn't fit down the disposal or couldn't be cut up and flushed down the toilet, she pretty much had to hang on to it. She had enough furniture crammed into her apartment to furnish Mama's and my place easily without ever making a dent in her own clutter. A lot of what we lived with was patched up or held together with duct tape, but as Bernadette said, there was no sense in tossing stuff out that was P.F.—perfectly fine.

Bernie asked Mama lots of questions after she found us, but even if Mama had understood the questions, Bernie quickly learned, she didn't have the words to answer them. The only information Bernadette could manage to get out of Mama was our names—Heidi and So Be It. That's what Mama told Bernie her name was, So Be It. Bernadette couldn't believe that was right, so she asked her again and again, but the answer was always the same. *So Be It.*

Mama couldn't read or write her name, so it was Bernie who decided how it should look on paper.

"Every person deserves to have a proper first and last name, and if there's a middle initial to plunk down between them, all the better," she said.

So Mama became So B. It, and her last name, strange though it was, became mine as well. It.

When I turned five, which is about the time most kids start kindergarten, I didn't go to school. Bernadette decided to keep me home and teach me herself. I never wondered why I wasn't doing what all the other five-year-olds were doing because I didn't know. I didn't know any other five-year-olds. In fact, I didn't know any kids at all. Except for Zander.

Zander was short for Alexander. He was a few years older than me, and he was fat. Bernadette told me it was rude to call people fat even if they were, but considering what he called me the first time I met him, I felt fine about it. I was downstairs taking out the trash.

"What's a *ree*-tard?" I asked Bernadette when I got back upstairs.

"In music it's pronounced rih-*tard*, short for the Italian *ritardando*, which means slowing down," she said.

"What does it mean when it's pronounced *ree*-tard and somebody says it about you in English?" I asked.

"It usually means the person saying it is a dimwit."

"Is Zander downstairs a dimwit?" I asked.

"I expect he is," she said.

Truthfully, Zander wasn't very smart, and because my first impression of him was that he wasn't very nice, either, I avoided him. Then one day on another trash run I came across him sitting on the stairs, and out of the blue he offered me a Twinkie from one of the two-packs he was eating. Bernadette didn't allow junk food in the house. She said it was a waste of money and, besides that, bad for your gray matter. Zander loved junk food. The junkier the better, which kind of proved her point I guess. Besides junk food, Zander also liked to squish ants between his fingers, but most of all he liked to talk.

Over time we developed a little ritual, Zander and I. We would meet downstairs every afternoon at three fifteen when he got home from school and hang out on the front stoop. There were a lot of things I didn't really like about Zander. He talked rough, he didn't always smell good, and I didn't like what he did to those ants, but I did like to listen to him talk.

The way it worked with us was that as soon as we sat down, Zander would give me a handful of whatever junk he was eating that day to keep me busy. Then he'd launch into one of his stories. He loved to tell stories. He had some favorites he'd tell over and over—like the one about finding a bag of hundred-dollar bills on the sidewalk and burying it in a butter cookie tin out in the woods. He also liked to brag about his father being a war hero.

Upstairs with Bernadette, talking was easy. We told each other what we thought or how we felt or something interesting we'd figured out. Words traveled in straight lines. But when Zander talked, nine times out of ten he was bending the truth to within an inch of its life. After each whopping fib, he'd say, "It's the God's truth, swear on my mother's spit," and I would solemnly nod to let him know I believed every word he had said.

I was no dummy—I knew Zander was lying like a rug, but I didn't want him to stop. I was fascinated by his fibbing. Bernadette had told me that people lie when the truth is too hard to admit, so each day as I sat there nibbling my snack with my eyes locked tight on Zander's face, I was only listening with half my brain. The other half was busy trying to figure out the truth.

Zander was in the third grade when I met him. He went to Scarlett Elementary over on the South Side. When Bernadette decided not to send me to school, she told me if anyone ever asked, I was to tell them I was being home-schooled.

We had "school" every morning at the kitchen table. In the very beginning Mama would sit with us too—especially when we were working on letters. But after a while I'd learned all my letters and my numbers, too, so while I moved on to other things, mornings became Mama's coloring time. Bernadette bought Mama all kinds of coloring books, and we had a big shoebox full of crayons. Mama loved to color. She didn't stay inside the lines and she only used one color for each drawing, but she was happy and it kept her occupied while Bernie taught me.

"Blue!" Mama would call out to us from the other room each time she finished a drawing.

"You go, Picasso!" Bernie would call back.

Mama used all the crayons—yellow and pink and my favorite color, purple, but no matter what color she used, she called it blue. Sometimes I worried that maybe the reason Mama only had one word for colors was that she only saw one color. It made me sad to think that Mama's world might have no pink or yellow or purple in it. But I knew Mama loved me even though she didn't have words to tell me, so I decided the same thing was true of the colors—just because she didn't have words for them didn't mean she couldn't see them.

In the afternoons, after "school," Mama and I often went out to do shopping and run errands. Bernadette would give us a list of things to do. Some of the words on the list would be spelled out in block letters—BREAD, MILK, EGGS—but if there was something I couldn't read yet, like Jujyfruits, she'd draw a little picture of it for me. At first we could only go places that didn't require crossing any streets, because neither Mama or I knew how to do that safely. Later Bernadette made us practice street crossing by laying towels across the kitchen floor and teaching us to look both ways before we walked over them. Mama was happy to hold my hand and she looked both ways too, but I could tell she didn't know what she was supposed to be looking for.

I got to know some nice people outside. The cashiers at the grocery store, Frances and Cathy, and later the librarian at the public library, Mrs. Coppleman. Sometimes when Mama and I were out, we would see kids who looked like they might be about my age. I remember thinking that it would have been nice to play with them, but whenever we stopped in the park to swing or to sit on the bench and feed bread crumbs to the squirrels, the kids would whisper and move away from us.

You couldn't really tell about Mama's brain just from looking at her, but it was obvious as soon as she spoke. She had a very high voice, like a little girl, and she only knew twenty-three words. I know this for a fact, because we kept a list of the things Mama said tacked to the inside of the kitchen cabinet. Most of the words were common ones, like *good* and *more* and *hot*, but there was one word only my mother said, *soof*.

"What do you think it means when she says it?" I would ask Bernadette.

"Only your mama knows that," she'd tell me each time I asked.

That word, *soof*, became like a little burr sticking in my head, pricking me so I couldn't forget it was there. I found myself thinking about it more and more.

"There must be some way to find out what it means," I'd say to Bernie.

"Not necessarily, Heidi."

"Well, it has to mean *something* or Mama wouldn't say it. She knows what it means."

"Maybe so, but that doesn't mean that you ever will. Believe me, Heidi, there are some things in life a person just can't know."

The thing is, I didn't believe her, and a lot was going to have to happen before I would.

Bernadette talked to my mother the same way she talked to her cats. It sounded almost like singing.

"Precious Bouquet! Where, oh where is my

Precious Bouquet?" she called every morning when she came through the connecting door to help me get Mama up and dressed.

Getting Mama going in the morning used to be hard, before she learned to brush her own teeth and comb her hair. It got easier along the way, except that it was always hard to predict when Mama was going to cook up a rimple or hoist a foible, as Bernie also sometimes called it. I think we both felt better knowing we had each other there just in case.

Precious Bouquet, or usually just Precious, is what Bernadette called Mama.

"If, God forbid, So Be It is her true given name, I hope to heaven I never meet the person who gave birth to a gentle soul like your mama and slapped a no-name kind of name on her like that. It's just plain cruel," Bernie said.

"Why is it cruel?" I asked.

"So Be It means the same thing as amen."

"Like in the Bible?"

"Yes. In fact, it's the very last word in the Bible. Amen. That's what you say when something's over and done with, Heidi."

"Sort of like *The End*?" I said.

"Exactly," said Bernadette. "So be it. The end. In my mind the beginning of a life, especially if it seems destined to be a challenging one, deserves the most promising name you can come up with. A beginning kind of a name. Like Dawn. Or Hope. Or Aurora."

"Is Heidi a promising name?" I asked.

She smiled at me and touched my cheek.

"Filled to the brim with promise," she said. "At any rate I imagine it was your mother's mother who had the sad notion to give your mama her name, and I'll tell you something: If ever I meet up with your grammy, I'm gonna give her such a piece of my mind."

I know it's strange, but until Bernadette mentioned my grammy like that, I hadn't thought to wonder if I had one. Bernie had always said it was as if Mama and I had dropped from the sky, and up until then I guess I just figured that we had.

"Has Mama got a mother?" I asked.

"Everybody's got a mother," she answered.

"Where is she then?"

"That's another question entirely," she said.

"What's the answer?" I asked.

Bernadette laughed.

"I'm not going to tell you there isn't one, because I know you well enough by now to know that'll get your panties in a twist, Heidi-Ho."

"People don't just disappear off the face of the earth without somebody noticing, do they?" I asked.

"Not usually, no," Bernadette said softly.

Bernadette was a big list maker, and once she had me reading and writing on my own, she got me into the habit of list making too. Mostly hers were shopping and to-do lists. Some of mine were like that too—ways of keeping track of things, like Mama's vocabulary list on the cupboard door, but I made other kinds of lists too. One of the very first ones I remember was called "Things I Know About Mama." There wasn't much to it.

Things I Know About Mama

Name: So B. It

Obviously, I wasn't much of a list maker back when I did that, because I certainly knew a lot more about my mother than just her name. I could have put down that she stood five feet tall on the dot in bare feet, and she had the same pale-blue eyes I do, only wider set. And I could've said she was beautiful and her hair was bone straight, not curly like mine, and parted in the middle so that it hung down like curtains on either side of her face. I knew other things too. Like she hated to wear socks, rainy days made her anxious, and she'd do almost anything you asked her to if you promised her a Jujyfruit after—as long as it wasn't a green one. I could have put all of that down, and more besides, but as I said, I wasn't much of a list maker back then. I kept my lists in a red spiral notebook with dividers, and sometimes I wish I still had it to remind me of who I was before.

After Bernadette brought up that business about my grammy giving Mama an unpromising name, I started thinking about some things I hadn't thought about before.

"Who am I?" I remember asking Bernadette one day in the kitchen.

"You are my sh-sh-sugar baby, my sugar baby doll," she sang in reply.

"No, Bernie. Who am I really?" I asked again.

"You're Heidi. Heidi It."

"Is that all?" I said.

"That's plenty in my book. What more do you need to be than who you are right now?"

"Shouldn't a person know their history?" I asked.

"What is it that you want to know?" Bernie said.

"Lots of things."

"Such as?" she said.

"Where was I born and who named me Heidi?" I asked.

"Maybe you were named after the book or maybe the movie. Shirley Temple was in that. Oh, how I loved her movies."

"But who saw the movie? Mama? My grammy?"

"What difference does it make?" Bernie said.

"A person isn't supposed to have to guess who they are, they're supposed to *know*," I said.

"You know who you are, Heidi, and you have a history, too."

"Not from the beginning," I said. "Only from when Mama and I met you."

"What happened before that doesn't matter, baby. It's just something to be grateful for, because if it hadn't happened, you and I wouldn't be standing here right now having this conversation."

"A person has a right to know from the beginning," I insisted.

"I suppose a person has a right to *want* to know," she said.

It wasn't too long after that that I decided to make a new list. Instead of things I knew about Mama, it would be a list of all the things I *didn't* know about her. There were so many, I had a feeling as I opened my notebook this would turn out to be the longest list I'd ever made. I pictured it being so long that it would stretch to the moon and back again.

I began in the usual way, by writing the heading on top—

Things I Don't Know About Mama

Then I wrote the first thing that came to mind—

What is soof?

And here's the funny thing: Once I wrote that, I couldn't go any further. I stared at the page for a long time, but all the other questions I'd thought of seemed small and unimportant compared to that one. *What is soof?* The words grew louder in my head, and as I watched, the letters expanded and blurred together, spreading across the page and spilling over the edges like sweet milky tea, until the question became so vast that I could imagine it stretching to the moon and back again all by itself.

CHAPTER FIVE

Shh

When I was very little, before I could go outside, we had to have everything delivered—groceries, clothes, everything. Mama couldn't shop by herself because she couldn't read or handle money, and I was way too young to go out alone with her. I think Bernadette liked it better that way—all of us staying inside together. Bernie was great on the phone—she could talk people into bending the rules and helping us out in all kinds of ways. Every now and then somebody wasn't willing to bring us whatever it was we needed, and when that happened, whatever it was, we just did without.

But Mama and I were the opposite of Bernadette. We wanted to go out. I used to sit on Mama's lap at the window, and we'd both laugh when the sparrows landed on the sill or when cars honked their horns below in the street. Once I was old enough, I began to beg Bernie to let Mama and me go out to do the shopping together. Eventually she gave in. At first we were only allowed to go places on our block, because of the street crossing thing. Luckily there was a Double D grocery store on the corner. Bernie would stand by the door wringing her hands the whole time we were gone, but Mama and I loved the Double D. We liked to push the cart down the aisles, and to taste the tiny sample cubes of yellow cheese or muffin they sometimes put out on the counters. On the way home Mama and I held hands and laughed out loud at the pigeons scurrying away from us as we walked. I loved being out with Mama. But all that changed the day the vacuum cleaner broke.

Our vacuum cleaner was an ancient metal tank with fins that looked like a rocket ship about to blast off. After it broke, Bernie called around and found out that nobody made that kind anymore and only one store in Reno had the part we needed to fix it. They wouldn't send the piece and it was too far away to walk, so I begged Bernie to let Mama and me take the bus.

"Pretty please with sugar on top?" I pleaded.

I had never taken a bus before, but I had seen them pass by under the window a million times and I was dying to ride on one. Bernie was reluctant, but I badgered her until finally she showed me out the window where the bus stop was and gave Mama and me enough change for two round trips.

"It's in a different neighborhood, Heidi. All strangers. Fly under the radar. Don't talk to anyone. Don't even look at them, and you hold your mama's hand the whole time. It's not safe, do you understand me?" she told me nervously. "It's not safe."

Mama and I walked down to the corner to wait for the bus. Despite all that Bernie had said, I wasn't afraid—I was excited. The Number Five commuter came around the corner and passed so close to us that it blew Mama's hair back away from her face and lifted her dress up above her knees. The brakes made a high-pitched screeching noise, or at least I thought that's what it was until I realized the sound was coming out of Mama's mouth.

She was screaming, and when she began to sob and clutch at her chest, I grabbed her arm and tried to pull her down the sidewalk toward home. Bernadette had seen and was hanging out the window yelling when we got there—

"Get inside, Heidi. Hurry up! Hurry up! Get inside."

People stopped to stare, and a woman in a big hat tried to grab my shoulder.

"Do you need help, little girl?" she asked. "Do you want me to call the police?"

Bernadette was waiting at the door with the Jujyfruits when we got upstairs, but Mama didn't even seem to see her. She rushed into the room and started walking in a circle, patting her chest rapidly with one hand.

"Done. Done. Done, Heidi, shh," she kept saying over and over.

Bernadette tried to give her Jujyfruits, but Mama wouldn't take them.

"Done. Done. Done, Heidi, shh," Mama said again.

"Why is she doing that?" I asked.

Bernadette watched her for a minute and then a sad, knowing look came over her face.

She went to Mama and said very softly:

"Why don't you give me the baby, Precious? She'll be safe with me. Give her to me now, okay?"

"What baby?" I asked. "What are you talking about, Bernie?"

"Give me the baby," she said again to Mama. "Give Heidi to me, Precious."

Mama stopped pacing. Breathing heavily, she slowly extended her arms to Bernadette, who reached out and took the invisible baby from her. As soon as she had done that, Mama went out to the kitchen and lay down in the middle of the floor. She curled up and shut her eyes.

"What's happening?" I asked Bernadette.

"I think maybe your mama's having a memory," she said.

"You said, 'Give me Heidi.' Is Mama remembering me?" I asked.

"I'm not sure, honeylamb."

Then Mama said something that neither of us could quite hear. I got down on the floor next to her and leaned over her, stroking her hair.

"What is it, Mama?" I whispered. "What do you remember?"

"*Soof*," she whimpered softly, "*soof.*"

How can you tell if someone has memories if they can't talk about the things they remember? Mama remembered lots of things from one day to the next—how to make tea, where her toothbrush was, how to open cans—but did she remember her past? Her mother? The day I was born? My father? Maybe she had pictures of all those memories in her head, but she didn't have the words to describe them. Or maybe her broken machine had a little hole in the side and all those memories had slipped through it like small round candies, rolling across the floor, into dark corners, or under the bed among the dust bunnies. All except one, that is. One memory was so important, Mama held on to it and gave it a word all its own to help her to remember . . . *soof.*

I spent hours picturing that word with all the answers to my unanswered questions tied to it, one after the other like the knotted rag tail of a kite. I'd imagine myself standing there on the ground holding on to the ball of string while that word sailed and skidded and danced across the cloudless blue sky above me.

But only Mama knew what it meant. And she wasn't telling.

"What is *soof*, Mama?" I'd whisper as I sat on the edge of her bed at night gently scratching her back. I hoped it might slip out of her mouth and onto her pillowcase as she closed her eyes and relaxed into the rhythm of my scratching.

Sometimes I'd sit down next to her on the couch, open up a magazine, and flip through the pictures, pointing at things—a baby, a dog, a car.

"Show me *soof*, Mama. Is this *soof* ? Is this?"

Mama would smile her sweet, wide smile and pat my knee the way she always did when I sat close to her.

"Tea, Heidi?" she'd say. "Tea?"

With anybody else I might've thought offering to get me tea right then like that was a way of changing the subject in order to avoid having to answer the question. Like the time Zander offered to let me see the wart on his foot when what I'd asked him to show me was one of the medals he claimed his father had won in Vietnam. But I knew Mama didn't understand what I was asking. She could tell that I wanted something, and she didn't want to disappoint me, so she offered me one of the only things she was sure she could give me. Tea. So I said, "Sure, Mama. I'd like some tea." And she said, "Good, Heidi. Tea," and went off to the kitchen to make us two cups of Lipton—hers in the white cup with the gold rim and mine in the one with pink roses, both with three spoons of sugar and a splash of milk, just the way Bernadette had taught her. But a million cups of Mama's sweet tea couldn't have washed away my longing for the meaning of that word.

Before Bernadette had come down with her A.P., she'd been a big fan of the library. She went there practically every day. I knew Bernie missed the library, so I was glad when I was finally allowed to walk the three and a half blocks to go there for her. Mama would come too. She liked to look at the picture books. Before we stopped going out together, Mama and I went to the library at least once a week.

Bernie made lists of the books she wanted me to take out for her to read, and she was also always having me look up things about hermit crabs or George Washington Carver or whatever else we happened to be studying at "school." Whenever I brought a new stack of books home, Bernie would press them to her nose, close her eyes, and breathe in deep, just like I'd seen her do with her father's old overcoat, which still hung in the hall closet in her apartment.

After I started wondering about *soof*, I asked Mrs. Coppleman, the librarian, if she'd ever heard of Mama's word, and she said it sounded like maybe it was foreign. She showed me where the international dictionaries were, and I looked in all of them. Nothing. I'd already looked it up at home in M.B.F., of course, hoping to run my finger down the page and find it there among the other *s-o-o* words. *Soon, soot, sooth, soothe. . .* It wasn't there. It wasn't anywhere, except in Mama's head.

I kept one ear cocked, listening for her to say it. On the rare occasions when she did, I'd pounce on it, looking for clues. Once she said it while she was watching Bernie brush the tangles out of my hair after a bath. Another time when she cut her finger on the lid of a can she was trying to open. But it wasn't consistent. I stood in front of her and brushed my hair a million times after that, trying to trigger it, but it didn't work. When it came, it came without rhyme or reason.

I began hearing it in strange places. Awake in the night during a rainstorm, cars passing by under the window, their wet tires whispering—*soof*. Bernie's slippers sometimes said it too as she shuffled across the speckled linoleum between the sink and the old round-shouldered refrigerator.

I spent hours looking into Mama's eyes, imagining that somewhere behind them was a little package all wrapped up for me with a tag attached saying, *This is soof.*

I started having trouble sleeping. Bernadette learned to steer clear of me when I was "under-slept"—she'd been around enough cranky old cats to know how to avoid being scratched and hissed at. But when my upset started rubbing off on Mama and making her rimply, Bernadette lost patience and lit into me.

"Heidi, I've said it before and I'll say it again: There are some things in life you just cannot know, and the meaning of that word of your mama's is one of them. The sooner you come to grips with that, the better it will be for all of us."

Maybe she was right. Maybe it was time to give up. Why did I think that word was so important, anyway? For all I knew, it was nonsense, some misremembered thing she'd overheard somebody say on the street. I told myself these things over and over, hoping to talk myself into believing them. Maybe I would have, too, if I hadn't found the camera way in the back of the sticky bottom drawer in the kitchen where we kept odds and ends like birthday candles and rubber bands. I was looking for the Scotch tape and yanked the drawer open so hard, the whole thing came crashing out onto the floor, and there it was. A black plastic Kodak Instamatic camera, and inside it a roll of film. Used.

My search for the truth began in earnest after I had that film developed. The day I came home with the pictures, Bernadette was sitting at the dining-room table looking at a library book about marsupials.

"Wish I had a pouch," she said. "Perfect for stashing reading glasses."

I set the envelope of photos down in front of her. She closed her book without even bothering to save the place.

"Tell the truth, Heidi," she said, picking up the yellow envelope and turning it over in her hands. "Did you peek at them on the way home? It's okay if you did."

"No. I was afraid to," I said.

"What's the worst it could be?" she asked.

"Nothing. The worst would be if there was nothing," I said.

"Well, let's see what there is then, baby," she said softly as she slid a finger under the flap and broke the seal. "Let's just see."

CHAPTER SIX

Tea

There were twenty-three photos in all. The same number as Mama had words. Some of the pictures were so blurry you couldn't tell what they were, but plenty of them were clear. They were all taken at a Christmas party. There was a dressed-up Santa Claus with a white cotton beard and a crooked tree covered with paper chains and glitter pinecones that looked homemade. Some of the people in the pictures were walking around with trays of punch and cookies and some were sitting in wheelchairs or slumped in orange and turquoise molded plastic chairs with thin metal legs.

"Who are all these people?" I asked, slowly examining each photo before slipping it to the back of the stack.

Bernie was sitting next to me on the couch,

her head bent toward mine.

"Looks like it could be some kind of a club, and this was their Christmas party," Bernie said.

"Why are so many of them twisted up?" I asked.

"Handicapped, you mean?" said Bernie. "Maybe it's a hospital or a special home."

"Who took the pictures?" I asked. "Do you think Mama did?"

"I doubt if she could use a camera, baby."

"Then who took them, and how did Mama end up with the camera?" I asked.

Bernie shook her head.

"I don't know, sweetie."

There were several pictures of a group of three plump teenaged girls with drooping eyelids and ill-fitting party dresses, then two of a shaggy-haired boy about eighteen or nineteen. His eyes were beautiful—dark blue, almost black—but his head seemed balanced at an odd angle on top of his thin neck, his mouth contorted in a grimace, which could have been either pain or pleasure, it was hard to tell. In one of the shots the man in the Santa suit stood beside the boy, his arm around his shoulder, neither one smiling. The Santa was extremely tall and thin, and he hadn't bothered to pad the suit, so it billowed out loosely around the middle. His street clothes—shirt collar, necktie, and pant cuffs—poked out from under the red-and-white costume, the sleeves so short that his bony wrists stuck out a good three inches from the white cuffs, revealing the gold watch he had on.

"Pretty scrawny-looking Santa," I said.

"It's not the missing belly of jelly that bothers me, it's what his eyes are saying," Bernie said.

"How can you tell under those big cotton eyebrows?" I asked.

"I can tell," she said.

After that, more snapshots of people posing in front of the tree and eating cookies, and then came a slightly blurry picture of a middle-aged blond woman in a red sweater with reindeer on it standing in front of a massive stone fireplace, with her arm around a smiling girl with wide-set pale-blue eyes. I knew right away the girl was Mama.

"She was kind of fat," I said.

"Or maybe she was pregnant," Bernie said.

"With me, you mean?" I asked, looking hard at the photo.

"Seems like a safe bet," she said, taking the picture from me and looking at it closely. "And my guess is that the woman in the red sweater is your grammy."

I grabbed the photo back from Bernadette and stared at the blond woman.

"Really? How do you know?"

"Look at the eyes. What do you think, Heidi?" asked Bernadette.

"They look like Mama's only not so wide apart."

"They look like *yours*, baby," Bernadette said gently.

We went through the whole stack of photos several times. Most of them were taken inside in the room where the party was, but there was one taken outdoors, on a wooden porch under a big sign with green letters that said *Hilltop Home, Liberty, New York*.

"We have to show the pictures to Mama as soon as she wakes up," I said excitedly. "She knew these people, Bernie! She was *there*."

"Yes, she was, baby. But you know how your mama is—she might not be able to recognize herself from a photograph. Especially an old one."

"Maybe looking at these will zap Mama's brain like a bolt of lightning and jump-start her memory, Bernie." Then it hit me. "Maybe *soof* is in the pictures!"

"Maybe," she said, but I could tell she had her doubts.

While Mama finished napping, I let myself float suspended like a lily pad in my private little pool of hope. I passed the time by looking up Liberty, New York, in the atlas and pressing my finger down again and again on the town where Hilltop Home had been—the place where my mama and maybe *my grammy* had stood in front of a big fireplace smiling at the camera. I wondered about who had taken the photographs, and how Mama and I had ended up so far from New York. I wondered where my grammy was now and whether Hilltop Home was still there, in Liberty. I was just about to go over to Bernie's and ask if we could call information to check for a listing when I heard Mama stir and call out.

Bernadette had gone back to her apartment to feed her cats, Clara Barton and Cookie Dough—named after one of her heroes and one of my favorite flavors of ice cream. The cats never came through the door into Mama's and my house. When they got hungry or lonely, they stood on the threshold and cried for Bernie. I used to worry that they did that because they had caught Bernie's A.P., but she assured me that it wasn't a catching thing—for animals or people.

When I heard Mama calling, I ran to the kitchen and shouted through the doorway, "Come quick, Bernie! She's up!"

Bernadette came right over and we went into Mama's room together. She was lying under her covers rubbing her eyes. When she saw us, she smiled.

"Hello, Heidi. Hello, Dette."

I remember the first time Mama called Bernadette "Dette." I thought Bernie was going to cry from sheer joy. Mama didn't add new words to her vocabulary very often, so each one was a big event in our house. That was a very special addition. It was number fifteen on the list.

"Hello, Precious," Bernadette cooed as she sat down on the bed next to Mama and pushed the hair out of her eyes. "How did you sleep? How is your head?"

Mama used to get a lot of headaches. She'd hold her head and rock and moan. Usually a nap would make it better, but sometimes she needed Tylenol. She had trouble taking any kind of pills—she couldn't swallow them—so Bernadette would grind up the tablets and put the powder in Jell-O. Mama loved Jell-O almost as much as Jujyfruits.

"Can we show her now?" I whispered.

"Shh, Heidi. Slow down. She's only just waking up, and her head was hurting pretty bad before she went to sleep. Give her a second."

I could barely contain myself as Bernadette sat by Mama, talking softly to her until she was awake enough to get up and go comb her hair and wash her face.

Finally Mama emerged from the bathroom and came to sit by me on the couch.

"Hello, Heidi," she said, patting my knee.

"Hello, Mama," I replied, trying to keep my voice calm and even.

I looked at Bernadette and she shrugged.

"Mama, do you want to see some pretty pictures?" I asked.

Mama nodded.

"They were taken a long time ago at Hilltop Home, Mama. Do you remember Hilltop Home?"

Mama smiled and patted my knee.

"Hello, Heidi," she said.

"Hello, Mama."

I picked up the stack of photographs and chose one, holding it carefully by the edges so I wouldn't smudge it.

"Look, Mama. See the Santa Claus?"

Mama looked at the photograph and smiled. I showed her another one.

"See all the people?"

Mama looked at the photograph and smiled. Bernadette came over and looked over my shoulder at the picture I was showing Mama.

"Don't they look pretty, Precious?" she asked.

Mama said, "Pretty, Dette."

"Look at this one, Mama. Who do you see?"

I showed her the photograph of the girl and the woman in the red sweater in front of the fireplace.

Mama looked at the photograph and smiled. "*Soof*," she said.

My heart nearly stopped.

"Where, Mama? Show me. Show me *soof*."

I was barely able to contain my excitement.

"Tea, Heidi?" Mama said suddenly, smoothing her skirt nervously with both hands.

"Wait, Mama. Not yet. First show me *soof*."

Mama began to smooth her skirt faster.

"Tea, Heidi?" she said, her voice rising up a notch.

"I don't want any tea, Mama. I want you to show me *soof*. Point to *soof*," I said.

I was talking louder than I meant to be, louder than I should have been, and I felt Bernadette reach out and squeeze my shoulder.

"Leave your mama be now, Heidi. She'll show us when she's ready to."

"No she won't," I said, shrugging out from

under Bernadette's hand and pulling Mama's hands roughly away from her skirt. I took her right hand tightly in my own, forced her index finger out straight and pressed it against the photo.

"Show me, Mama. Where is *soof*?"

"That's enough, Heidi," said Bernadette.

"Show me, Mama," I demanded.

"Uh-oh. Uh-oh," Mama repeated anxiously, wriggling as she tried to escape my grip. "Tea, Heidi? Tea?"

"I don't want any tea!" I shouted. "I want you to tell me, Mama! I want to *know*."

Mama whimpered.

"Done, done, done, Heidi, shh," she said.

"Leave your mama be, Heidi," Bernadette said sternly.

"You're not ever going to tell me, are you, Mama?" I shouted, ignoring Bernadette. "Are you, Mama? Are you?"

I let go of her hand and angrily ripped the photo in half, throwing the pieces in Mama's lap. Then I ran to my room, slammed the door, and with a jagged sob flung myself face-down on the bed.

I cried for a long time. I cried so hard, it felt like my ribs might crack open. I imagined my heart flying out like a small, red bird escaping its cage, going off in search of a more promising person to live in. A person with a history. A person who *knew*.

After a while I heard my door open and Bernadette and Mama come in.

"Your mama's made some tea for you, Heidi. Just the way you like it. Sit up, baby, and take it from her, will you please? She needs you to," Bernadette said quietly.

I dried my eyes and sat up. Mama looked so worried and sad standing there with my white cup with the pink roses in her hand. I took it from her and tried to smile.

"Thank you, Mama. Thank you for the tea."

"Good, Heidi, tea," she said, brightening immediately. Then she turned and walked out of the room.

"Where are you going, Precious?" Bernadette called after her.

Mama reappeared a second later holding the two halves of the photograph I'd torn.

"Uh-oh," she said, handing me the pieces. "*Soof.*"

Slowly I got up off the bed and went and stood beside her.

"Which one, Mama? Which one is *soof*? This one?" With my right hand I held out the piece of the photograph that showed Mama as a young girl. "Or this one?" I asked, holding out the other piece of the photo.

Mama looked at me and smiled. Then she reached over and clumsily pushed the two pieces together.

"Tea, Heidi?" she said.

CHAPTER SEVEN

Out

Until I had that old roll of film developed and saw the sign with the green letters on it hanging over the porch, I had never heard of Liberty, New York. It's not exactly a famous place. Just a small town in the Catskill Mountains, about two and a half hours northwest of New York City. But because I knew that my mother and maybe my grandmother too had been there, suddenly it became the most important place in the world to me.

If Mama truly was pregnant with me in the picture, that meant the photos had been taken almost thirteen years earlier. I was afraid that Hilltop Home wouldn't still be there, but Bernadette got the number from information without any problem and we called them up.

I stood next to Bernadette firing questions

at her a mile a minute as she spoke to the person on the other end of the phone.

"Ask them if Mama lived there! Tell them she was at a big Christmas party maybe with her mother."

Bernadette tried to ask all those questions and more, but for some reason the person on the other end wouldn't let her finish a sentence.

"Yes, I understand, but if you could just tell me if . . . Yes, I see, but all we really need you to do is look in your records—is that too much to . . . Uh-huh. Okay, okay."

Finally Bernadette gave her phone number and hung up.

"What happened? What did they say?" I asked.

"About all I managed to get out of her was that Hilltop is a home for handicapped people and the only person authorized to answer personal questions about it is somebody named Thurman Hill."

"Then we need to talk to Thurman Hill right away," I said.

"He isn't there today. She took my number and said he'd call me back."

But Thurman Hill didn't call back. Not that day. Or the next.

So Bernadette called again. And again. Every time, she got the same runaround about how Mr. Hill was the only one who could answer our questions only he wasn't ever there. Bernadette called back so many times, finally the woman at Hilltop started putting her on hold as soon as she heard Bernie's voice, and then she'd just leave us hanging like that and never come back.

"Long distance is expensive, Heidi-Ho, and Thurman Hill, that miserable four-letter-word, clearly doesn't intend to return our phone calls."

Bernadette never swore in front of me, so when she got really mad, she substituted "four-letter-word" for the real four-letter curses. I knew all the real ones from Zander anyway—I'd even made a list of them in code in my notebook.

"I think it's time for a postal approach," she said.

Bernadette had had a lot of practice getting what she wanted by talking to people on the phone or writing them letters, but no matter what she did, she couldn't get anywhere with Hilltop. Three weeks passed and still we had no answers to our letters or calls. I was beside myself. Bernie tried to distract me by keeping my hands busy. We put new shelf paper in the kitchen cabinets, and one weekend she set me to cleaning out all the closets in our apartment. I was on my hands and knees pulling out boxes and squashed shoes and a battered old suitcase from the back of Mama's closet when I felt something soft wadded up in the far corner under a stack of old magazines. It was a moth-eaten red sweater. The same red sweater with reindeer on it that the blond woman in the photograph at Hilltop Home had been wearing.

"She was here, Bernie!" I cried, holding up the crumpled sweater for her to see. "My grammy was here. There's proof."

After that there was no distracting me. I couldn't think about anything but Hilltop.

"All we're asking them to do is just look up Mama's name in the files. Why is that so hard?" I asked.

"I don't know, baby, but it makes me so mad, I'd like to march right into Thurman Hill's stuffy old office and sit on the little piss-ant until he coughs up the information."

"That's it, Bernie!" I said, jumping up excitedly. "That's exactly what we have to do. We have to go see Thurman Hill! We have to go there and make him tell us about Mama."

"Baby," Bernadette said softly, "you know we can't do that. I can't—"

"Go out? How do you know? How do you know you can't?" I asked. "When's the last time you tried, Bernie? Maybe the A.P. is gone. Maybe you're better and you just don't know it."

"It's not gone, Heidi. Things don't just go."

"Colds do. And pimples. How do you know A.P. doesn't just go too? Maybe it does. Maybe it has," I said.

I was really excited now. I went to the front door and pulled it wide open.

"Come on, Bernie, try, please try. *For me.*"

"Heidi, I can't," Bernadette said. Her voice was tight and I noticed her hands trembling.

"You make Mama try. That's why she can open cans, Bernie, and comb her hair. You make me try too. Cursive, Bernie. Shakespeare, you made me try. That's all I'm asking you to do. Try."

Bernadette stood up, grasping the arm of the couch for support. Her legs wobbled under her, but she made her way slowly toward me. Toward the open door.

"I don't know . . ." she said. "You don't understand, Heidi. If I go out . . . If I'm out-side I might . . . if I go out . . ."

"Nothing will happen, Bernie. Just one step into the hall. That's all you have to do. One step. The *first* step. Like when you taught me the cursive *a*, remember? 'Round the block, up, down, curl the tail onto the next.' You can do it, Bernie. I know you can."

Bernadette took hold of the doorknob, her knuckles white with fear. She stood like that for a minute with her eyes closed tight.

"Round the block, up, down, curl the tail onto the next," she whispered under her breath. "Round the block, up, down, curl the tail onto the next." Then she took a deep breath, let go of the doorknob, and stepped out into the hall.

"You did it!" I shouted. "You're out, Bernie! I knew you could do it. You're out!"

The best way to describe what happened next is that in the few seconds between when Bernadette let go of the knob and when she collapsed on the floor, her body went from solid to liquid. Her legs juiced out from under her and she fell in a heap, her breath coming loud and fast, her eyelids fluttering as her head rolled backward like a broken doll's.

"Bernie!" I cried, rushing to her.

"Save me," she managed to whisper between gasps. "I'm . . . drowning."

I stood behind her, taking hold of her under the arms and trying with all my might to pull her back inside, but she was too heavy. Bernie was short but not small. "Peasant stock," she always said. "Low to the ground and built for business."

"Help me, Heidi," she groaned.

I heard a door scrape open below us, and familiar heavy footsteps on the stairs.

"Zander," I screamed. "Hurry! Up here. We need help!"

A minute later Zander's pasty round face peered around the top of the staircase. He was out of breath from climbing the one flight up. He had a bag of barbecue chips in one hand and a grape soda in the other. His jaw dropped when he saw Bernadette on the floor.

"Jeez," he said. "Whatsa matter with her?"

"Hurry. Help me pull her inside," I said.

He didn't move, just stood there nervously licking his spicy red fingertips.

"Man, she's white," he said. "Like a freakin' ghost."

"Zander, come *on*," I cried. "Help me get her inside."

Zander sighed and put his chips and soda down. Then he came and took one of Bernie's arms in his hands.

"She's not gonna croak, is she?" he whispered. "'Cause I never seen nobody croak in real life."

I grabbed Bernie's other arm and started pulling. One leg of her stockings caught on a nail on the floor and ripped loudly as we tugged. She moaned and went completely limp, which made her feel even heavier, but somehow eventually we managed to drag her across the welcome mat back inside.

"She don't look so good. Do you want me to call 911?" he asked.

I was terrified. If we called 911, they'd come and take Bernie away. What would Mama and I do? How would we survive without Bernie? I started to cry.

Zander stood for a minute looking down at Bernie's still body and shifting uncomfortably from foot to foot.

"Is she drunk?" he asked. "'Cause if that's what it is, I can tell you she won't wake up for a while and when she does, you gotta keep real quiet and make her drink hot coffee even if she cusses you out for it. You got coffee?"

"Yes, but she's not drunk," I said, wiping my nose on my sleeve.

"It's okay, I won't tell nobody," he said.

I felt a sliver of truth slip under my skin. A jagged little splinter of what lay underneath all those tales about war heroes and medals of honor.

Bernie stirred and moaned. Zander quickly knelt down next to me, and we both fanned her furiously with our hands as she came around.

"Please be okay," I whispered. "Please, Bernie, come back."

It seemed like forever before the color returned to Bernie's face and she opened her eyes. I sat beside her on the floor the whole time, stroking her arm and talking softly to her the way she always did with Mama when she was waking up from one of her headache naps. When Bernadette was finally able to sit up, I sat cross-legged and scooched very close, putting one arm around her and pressing her head against my shoulder while I rocked gently back and forth. Some of her long gray hair had come loose from the thick rope of braid she always wore, and I smoothed it away from her face, tucking it back into the weave.

"Done, done, done, Bernie, shh," I whispered.

Zander propped himself up against the door and watched. He didn't say or do anything more after that, but it was enough that he stayed. When Bernie was able to sit up and drink some water, he left, closing the door quietly behind him. I'd spent hours with Zander, listening to him tell stories out on the stoop, but until that day I hadn't really known him. Then, just like with the first pack of Twinkies he'd given me, without my asking, he handed me a tiny scrap of truth. After that everything changed. He would never be fat, or dim-witted, in my eyes again. I was only just beginning to see how powerful the truth could be.

Luckily Mama was asleep when the incident with Bernadette happened. I'm not sure how she would have reacted if she'd seen Bernie all fallen to pieces like that. I know it scared me down to the roots.

"I'm sorry, baby," she said. "I tried."

"I know you did, Bernie. It's okay," I told her. "I shouldn't have asked you to."

After a while we went into the kitchen and Bernie tried to make herself a cup of coffee, but she was still pretty shaky.

"Sit down, Bernie. I'll do it for you," I said.

Bernadette sat down heavily on one of the kitchen chairs and watched me grind beans in the coffee mill, an old beat-up wooden box with a crank on the top and a drawer in the bottom where the ground coffee fell in. I loved to pull open the drawer and smell the mysterious dark-brown powder, but I hated the bitter taste. I preferred Mama's sweet tea. Bernadette drank five cups of coffee every day—three in the morning, one after lunch, and one at five o'clock, which she called the cocktail hour.

"It's the devil's brew, Heidi. One sip and you're a goner."

"You're not gone," I'd say.

"True enough, but I'm a slave to the bean, Heidi. Trust me, a slave."

While we waited for the water to boil, I sat down across from her at the table.

"We won't give up on Hilltop, Heidi. I promise. We'll keep after them," she said. "We'll call and write until somebody up there gives us some answers. We will."

But I knew in my heart that wasn't going to work. Thurman Hill clearly planned to let us swing in the breeze. When I looked over at Bernie, still pale and shaken from her single step outside, I knew there was only one thing to do.

"Bernadette, I'm going to Liberty," I said.

"You? You mean *alone*?" she said incredulously. "That is totally out of the question. You're just a baby."

"I'm not a baby, I'm twelve. I go out by myself all the time," I said.

"Not to New York, you don't."

"I can fly there," I said.

"Have you lost your senses, girl?"

"People fly all the time, Bernie. All those planes we hear going by every day are filled with people."

"Other people, *strangers*, but not you. You're not like them," she said.

"No, Bernie, I'm not like *you*," I said hotly. "You and Mama are the ones who match."

Color rose in her cheeks, and her back visibly stiffened.

"I would no more let you get on an airplane than I would cut off my own foot," she said.

"Fine. I'll take a bus. It'll be cheaper anyway."

"Bus or plane, it makes no difference. You're not going," she said. "And that's the end of the discussion."

Bernie had a stubborn streak that ran the length of her spine like the white stripe on a skunk. She'd taught me pretty much everything I knew. But there was one thing I knew that Bernie didn't. I was going to Liberty.

CHAPTER EIGHT

More

I didn't tell Bernie about my plan. We both had our minds made up in opposite directions about me going to Liberty, and I didn't see any point in discussing it with her anymore. Anyway, she had her hands full with Mama, whose headaches were coming on a daily basis now. I might have told Zander, but he made himself scarce for a while after the incident with Bernie.

I called Greyhound from a phone booth outside and found out two important things. One, it would cost me $313 for a round-trip ticket to Liberty, and two, you had to be fifteen years old to travel across the country by yourself. As I've mentioned before, I was tall for my age, but the difference between twelve and fifteen is pretty noticeable, especially if you're looking for it.

Getting the money was the easy part. I won it playing a slot machine in the downtown Reno bus station. Since the machines at the Sudsy Duds only took nickels, I figured I should find one that took quarters so I wouldn't have to deal with quite so much change.

I wondered whether my sweet way with slots would extend beyond the realm of the Sudsy Duds, and luckily I found it did. I knew $313 in quarters would be a pretty heavy load, which is why I decided to look for a machine right in the bus station. That way I wouldn't have to haul the money too far. I took the Number Five bus there, crullered my own hair as best I could, and put on some of Bernadette's red lipstick in front of the cracked mirror in the station bathroom. Up close I wasn't very convincing, but I'd had plenty of practice flying under the radar.

It took me a little over half an hour to win the money off a big machine I found near a fast-food joint called Tommy Bun's Hotdog Heaven. I nearly had a heart attack when the coins started chunking down into the bin. They seemed so big and loud compared to the nickels I was used to at the Sudsy Duds. It was early in the morning and nobody was around to pay attention, so I squatted down next to the machine and counted out my winnings. Twelve hundred fifty-six quarters. One dollar more than I needed.

I had stopped at Bernie's bank on the way and gotten some paper sleeves to put the quarters in. Ten dollars' worth in each roll. It took me a long time to count and roll them all. When I was finished, I put the money into a big old canvas duffel bag I'd found in the back of one of the closets Bernie had made me clean out the week before.

I dragged the bag across the floor a little ways, to a bench near the ticket windows. It was too heavy to drag all the way back over to the bathroom, so I wiped off the lipstick with the back of my hand and unpinned my hair, using my fingers to comb out the biggest tangles. Then I sat and waited for the right person to come along and help me buy my ticket.

It didn't take long. She was kind of beat-up looking, with frizzy dark hair and black eyeliner all the way around her eyes. Her lips were thin and turned down at the corners in what could have seemed like a mean way, except I had a feeling she was okay underneath. Bernie probably would have found something wrong with what her eyes were saying, but I had to use my own judgment and she seemed all right to me. She sat down two benches away from me, her legs sticking straight out in front of her, snapping her gum and reading a magazine. I walked over, dragging the bag behind me, and got right to the point.

"I need somebody to buy me a ticket," I told her.

"Running away, are ya?" she said. "Boy, I know what that's all about, kiddo. Do I ever. But I ain't got no money for a ticket out of here. Not for you or me neither."

I didn't bother to explain to her that I wasn't running away—she probably wouldn't have believed me anyway.

"I've got the money." I opened the bag and showed her the rolls of quarters.

"Jeez Louise, whadja do, rob a piggy bank?" She laughed. Her teeth were crooked and the front left one was chipped and gray. "So alls you need is for me to buy it for you? How come you can't buy it yourself? You got enough money, right?"

I nodded.

"I'm not old enough to ride alone," I explained.

"How old you gotta be?" she asked.

"Fifteen," I said.

"You could be thirteen," she said, squinting at my face, "but not fifteen."

"I know. When I get on the bus, I'm going to ask somebody to let me pretend I'm with them. That way the driver won't ask me how old I am."

She smiled.

"You got a plan, don't ya? I like that. Girl with a plan. Hey, you maybe got enough to take me along?" she asked, arching a plucked eyebrow and eyeballing the rolls of quarters.

"No, sorry. All the extra I've got is these. You can have them, though." I fished around in my pocket and held out the four extra quarters I'd won.

She gave a crooked smile and shook her head.

"Keep it, kiddo. Where you looking to get to anyway?" she asked.

"Liberty."

"I hear you. Where are you going really, though?" she said.

"Liberty," I said again. "It's in New York."

"Oh. Never heard of it. So what's in Liberty?" she asked.

"I won't know for sure until I get there," I said.

She smiled again.

"You're pretty deep for somebody so low to the ground," she said. "Come on, let's go get you a ticket."

She helped me drag the duffel bag to the ticket window. I had been right about her being the right person, because I don't think many people would have been willing to stand there being chewed out by the ticket man for buying a ticket with all those quarters. Judi— she told me she was Judi with an *i*—didn't even flinch; she just stood there snapping her gum, saying, "Hey, money is money, man," and waiting until he finally shoved the ticket through the window at her.

"Get lost," he said as she turned away from him and handed me the ticket.

"Get a life," she replied over her shoulder.

I thought about Judi saying that and about how the way she said it made it sound insulting. But later, after I'd thanked her and was standing at the Number Five bus stop with my ticket to Liberty and the four extra quarters in my pocket, I found myself saying it softly under my breath: "Get a life, Heidi. Get a life," and there was something about the sound of it that I liked a lot.

CHAPTER NINE

Back Soon

Even if Bernadette hadn't had A.P., she wouldn't have been able to come with me on my trip. There's no way we could have brought Mama along, being the way she was about buses, and who else could have possibly taken care of her while we were away? I would have had to go alone no matter what.

I didn't tell Bernie the morning I went down to the bus station to play the slots and get my ticket. She thought I'd gone to the library. It was the first time I'd ever lied to her. I didn't like the way lying made me feel, so I was anxious to set it straight as soon as I got home. When I told her what I'd done and showed her the ticket, she was livid.

"I've poured my whole self into you, Heidi," she said, "like warm milk into a bucket.

Why are you doing this now? Why can't you just let things be?"

"Because things aren't the way they're supposed to be," I said.

"How are they supposed to be?" she asked.

"A person is supposed to know where they came from, Bernie."

"We've been over this already," she said. "It doesn't matter where you came from; it only matters that you're here."

"Maybe that's what matters to you, but I'm not like you, Bernie. I don't want to be like you, and I don't want to be like Mama either."

"Are you trying to hurt me, is that what this is all about?" she asked.

"It has nothing to do with you, Bernie. It's about *me*, don't you get it?" I shouted. "You think I'll forget about *soof* and Hilltop and all the rest of it, you *want* me to forget, but I won't. If I do, I'll end up like Mama—full of missing pieces."

"The pieces you're missing are not important ones, Heidi," Bernie said.

"Don't tell me what's important!" I yelled. "You don't know. You don't know anything.

You want me to be like you, but if you really cared about me you'd want me to be *normal*," I said.

Bernie turned her face away sharply as if she'd been slapped.

"I feel as though I don't even know you anymore," she said, and burst into tears.

I cried then too. Partly because I felt bad about hurting her feelings, but mostly because I realized that what she'd just said was true. She didn't really know me anymore. I wasn't sure I knew myself. I wanted to go to Liberty, I needed to go, but I was also afraid, and I couldn't admit my fear to Bernie—she would have pounced on it like a cat on a yarn ball, unwinding my resolve.

"It's not safe, Heidi," she said. "You're too young to go by yourself."

I didn't tell her that it also wasn't legal. Why should I fuel her fire when I knew she'd find out soon enough anyway?

"I have to go alone. You can't come with me and neither can Mama. There isn't any choice," I said.

"Yes, there is. Don't go." Bernadette was

begging now. "Wait until you're older. Listen to me. I'm not saying forget about it, I'm saying give it time. We can keep calling Hilltop. We can keep showing your mama the photographs. Maybe she'll remember something."

"You're just saying that to try to keep me here. You know Mama can't remember things, Bernie," I said. "I don't care what you say, I'm going."

"You may not go to Liberty and that is final, Heidi," Bernie said one last time.

"You're not my mother," I shouted. "You can't tell me what to do. You're not even family. You're nobody. *Nobody!*"

Bernie snatched the ticket out of my hand. She was so angry, she didn't even look like herself anymore.

"Is this what you want, Heidi?" she hissed through clenched teeth, her hand shaking as she held the ticket up in front of me. "Is this all that matters to you anymore?"

"Yes," I said.

She looked at me hard and long.

"Fine. Then go. Just go," she said.

She threw the ticket on the floor and

stomped across the kitchen and through the doorway into her apartment, slamming the door behind her. It's the only time I remember ever seeing that door closed.

Bernie and I didn't speak to each other for the rest of that day. I kept going out into the kitchen to check, but the door stayed closed, and for some reason I couldn't bring myself to open it. Mama asked for Dette several times, but I was able to distract her and keep her occupied with a Flintstones coloring book and endless cups of tea.

At dinnertime Bernie finally came over and heated up a can of stew. She spooned it onto plates for Mama and me, but she took her own plate back to her place. This time she left the door ajar.

I put Mama to bed alone for the first time in my life. Luckily she didn't give me a hard time. I even got her to shower and wash her hair, which was usually Bernie's department. Later I took my bath, and when I was lying in bed, Bernie came in and sat on the very edge of the bed.

"You mustn't lie to me ever again, Heidi," she said.

"I had to, Bernie. Otherwise you would have tried to stop me from getting the ticket," I said, raising up on one elbow and squinting at her in the dark.

I saw her smile a sad smile and shake her head a little.

"We both know I can't stop you, don't we, Heidi-Ho?"

Three days later, on the afternoon of September 22, I left for Liberty. I had tracked down Zander earlier in the day to say good-bye and to tell him that I'd managed to convince Mrs. Chudacoff that he would make a good replacement baby-sitter for me. He was happy about getting the job, but mostly he wanted me to tell him again and again exactly what I'd said about him to Mrs. C.

"I told her you were a good person," I said, "and a good friend."

"For real you said I was a good person? Swear on your mother's spit?" he said each time.

"Swear on my mother's spit," I promised.

"Cool." He beamed.

"Will you check in on Bernie and Mama?" I asked him. "Take out the trash and bring up the mail?"

"Yeah. You're coming back though, right?" he said.

I nodded and was a little surprised by how sad I felt about having to say good-bye to him.

Mama was in bed that day with one of her headaches. Bernie had already given her four Tylenols, but she was still moaning and holding her head.

"Good-bye, Mama," I said as I leaned over her to kiss her cheek.

"Back soon, Heidi?" Mama said, looking up at me.

"Yes, Mama. Back soon."

The trip itself would take three and a half days in each direction, but that wouldn't make any difference to Mama. She had no sense of time passing at all. I could have just as easily been going downstairs to check the mail that day. I stood at her bedside with Bernie's old beat-up P.F. blue suitcase in one hand, my backpack, containing my list book and two ham and cheese sandwiches, slung over my shoulder, and the ticket to Liberty carefully tucked into my jacket pocket.

"Back soon, Heidi?" Mama asked again, lifting her head off the pillow and smiling weakly at me.

"Yes, Mama," I replied.

But the truth was, I would not be back at all. Not as the same person I was that day, anyway.

Bernie and I had made up after our big fight. She told me that she forgave me for the angry things I'd said, and even though I promised not to lie to her again, there was something changed between us, and I carried the weight of knowing that I had hurt her. It was impossible for her to hide her fear about my trip, but she knew my mind was made up and didn't fight me anymore, not even when she found out about the age limit.

"I'll manage it," I told her, even though I wasn't sure how I would.

Bernie even helped me pack. Sometimes it almost felt as though we were on the same side, but then she'd say something that made it clear again how totally against the whole thing she was.

"This is all Thurman Hill's fault," she said bitterly right before I left Reno. "If he had just been willing to talk to us on the phone, you wouldn't be leaving now to go chase down that good-for-nothing four-letter word."

Her face went sad and she looked like she was about to cry.

"This is for you, Bernie," I said quickly, pulling a small cardboard tube out of my backpack and handing it to her.

"What's this?" she asked, wiping her eyes with the back of her hand. She opened one end of the tube and slid out the shiny rolled-up paper inside.

It was a map I had bought for her. I'd used a highlighter to mark the bus route from Reno to Liberty. There was another part to the gift, a plastic box of colored pushpins.

"The map is to put on the wall by the phone, Bernie. I'll call you at each stop, and you can use the pushpins to mark how far I've gone. You'll know exactly where I am that way, just like you always have."

Bernie hugged me.

"I have something for you, too," she said.

She handed me a small box tied around with red yarn.

"Open this when you get on the bus," she said.

We hugged again. Mama came out of her room still in her nightgown, her hair tangled and matted with sweat. I could tell from the way she was squinting that her head was still hurting.

"Kiss," Mama said, coming over and putting her arms around both of us, pressing her way into Bernie's and my embrace. I turned and pressed my cheek against her soft, smooth face. Mama felt my tears.

"Uh-oh, Heidi," she said.

"I love you, Mama," I said, and kissed her. Mama pulled away.

"Tea, Heidi?" she said, looking at me expectantly.

"No, Mama. No tea now."

"Ow, Dette," she said, holding her head.

"I know, Precious. I'll tuck you back in when Heidi goes, and you can have more Jell-O," Bernie told her. Then she turned to me. "You'll call from every stop?"

"Yes, from every stop," I promised.

"And I want you to call me the second you get to Liberty," Bernie said, putting her hands on my shoulders, the way she always did when she wanted to make sure I was listening to her.

"I will. I promise," I told her.

"You've got your sandwiches and the money I gave you?"

"Yes," I said.

"You remember the name of the cab company?" she asked.

"Yes, Bernie. ABC."

She had called Liberty information and located a cab service right near the bus stop that could take me up to Hilltop Home. She tried to let them know at Hilltop that I was coming, but the woman who answered the phone there kept putting her on hold before Bernie could get it out.

"You'll call me when you get to Liberty and then again when you reach Hilltop."

"Yes, Bernie," I told her again, "I promise."

"Don't tell anyone that you're traveling alone. You pretend to be with someone at all times. Someone who looks safe. A woman. Someone who could be your mother."

We'd been over these details countless times.

"Once you're at Hilltop, you get whatever answers there are to be gotten, Heidi, then climb right back on the bus and come home to us."

"I will," I said. She was still holding me by the shoulders, and when I tried to pull away, she slid her hands down my arms and took both my hands in hers.

"I have to go now, Bernie," I said.

Reluctantly Bernadette let go of my hands, and her arms fell heavily to her sides.

"Don't be afraid," she whispered.

"I'm not," I lied, even though I'd promised never to do that to her again.

"Heidi—" Bernie's voice got thick and her eyes filled up again.

"Don't worry, Bernie. I'll be fine."

"You're going now," she said.

It wasn't a question but a statement of fact.

When I got downstairs, I stood on the stoop and looked up. Bernadette and Mama were both standing at the window. Zander was sitting on the steps eating Devil Dogs. He handed me two unopened packs.

"For the road," he said.

I wanted to hug him, but I wasn't sure how he'd feel about that, so instead I punched him in the arm. He grinned and punched me back, but not too hard.

"See ya," he said.

I walked backward, my suitcase bumping against my leg, the box from Bernie tucked under my arm, waving to Mama and Bernie and Zander until I had to turn the corner. As I waited for the Number Five, I set my suitcase and the box down on the curb. I was really doing this. I was going to New York by myself. I felt a strange hollow sensation in the pit of my stomach and my mouth tasted funny, metallic like the water from the drinking fountain at the library. I swallowed hard and looked up at the clear blue sky. It was comforting to know that a piece of that very same sky would be hanging over Liberty when I finally got there. Bernadette had been right, I was going to Liberty to chase down a four-letter word—s-o-o-f.

CHAPTER TEN

Go

I got to the bus station with plenty of time to spare. I had planned to use the time to do what Bernie and I had agreed on, scout around for a woman sitting near my departure gate who I could get on the bus with. Once I got there, though, for some reason, that didn't feel right. There were plenty of women around, all shapes and colors and sizes, and a lot of them looked pretty friendly, but instead of picking one out, I found a seat on an empty bench and sat down. I sat there for almost forty-five minutes with my suitcase clamped between my knees, waiting. I don't know how to explain it—it was just a feeling I had that the right person would come along and find me instead of the other way around.

About fifteen minutes before my bus was due to leave, a woman in a long green raincoat came and sat down beside me. She had a little soft-sided suitcase with netting on the ends. Inside were five kittens, all different colors and patterns. They were mewing up a storm, so she was clicking her tongue and whispering to them to be quiet.

"They're scared is all, poor babies. It's the first time they've been away from their mama," she told me.

Her name was Alice Wilinsky, and she was on her way to a big family reunion in Salt Lake City. She was bringing the kittens along to give them away to some of her cousins, since she already had three cats at home, including the mama cat, Bebe. We started talking about cats and I told her about Cookie Dough and Clara Barton, and before I knew it they announced our bus and we got on together. Just as easy as that.

The first hour I was on the bus, Alice kept up a steady stream of chatter while I kept eyeing the box that Bernie had given me. I wanted to know what was inside. I didn't want to open it in front of Alice, though, in case it was something embarrassing. Finally nature called and she made her way to the rear of the bus to use the bathroom. I quickly untied the yarn and opened the box.

Inside was the red sweater. The one I'd found wadded up in the back of the closet. Bernie had washed and blocked it and carefully mended all the moth holes with matching red yarn. I'd had no idea she'd been working on it; she must have been doing it in her room at night after I'd gone to sleep. I slipped the sweater over my head and double rolled the sleeves up. It was much too big for me, but I didn't care. It was perfect. Soft and warm, and smelling wonderfully of home.

Home. I didn't dare let myself think about it. I was afraid that if I did, the hollow feeling that had taken hold in my stomach earlier would take over the rest of my insides and turn me wrong side out. To keep my mind off things, I got out my notebook and started a new list.

Things I Have Never Seen Before

cows
seats with footrests
roadkill 1) dead deer
           2) dead raccoon
           3) dead skunk
           4) mystery fur

Alice came back from the bathroom, and for a change she didn't seem to feel like talking. Instead she put up her footrest and pushed her seat back as far as it would go so she could nap. I wasn't tired yet, so I sat there working on my list for a while longer. I added three more things:

tollbooths
someone changing a flat tire
hitchhikers

The kittens were asleep in their bag tucked under Alice's seat, but after a while one of them woke up and began to cry. I got down and crouched between the seats, peering through the net at its tiny face.

"Don't worry," I whispered. "We'll be there soon."

We made our first stop at about seven o'clock that night in Fernley, Nevada. Alice didn't wake up, so I climbed over her, got off by myself, and called Bernie collect according to the plan. She cried when she heard my voice. I thanked her over and over for the sweater and quickly told her about the bus and about Alice and the kittens and everything else I could squeeze into our brief conversation. We'd agreed beforehand to set Bernie's egg timer each time I called to keep the calls down to five minutes; that way the bill wouldn't mount up too high.

She told me what she and Mama had been doing.

"We dusted today, Heidi. You know how your mama loves dusting."

Mama and Bernadette would always tickle each other with the feather dusters, so it was more of a game than a household chore, although I never noticed any dust around so I guess it accomplished more than just enter-taining Mama.

"How's her head?" I asked.

"She lay down for a couple of hours this afternoon after you left," she said, "and she's been fine since then. Are you okay? I've been so worried."

Bernie had put the map up in the kitchen next to the phone, and she stuck in the first pushpin, a blue one on Fernley. The timer dinged just as they announced my bus.

"Call me from your next stop," Bernie said. "That will be Lovelock."

"It's going to be pretty late," I said.

"I'll be up," she told me.

Bernie had given me fifty dollars before I left—it was all she could spare. I had the bills (which she had washed, of course) in my backpack. We knew that the cab to Hilltop would be fifteen dollars each way, so that meant I had only twenty dollars extra to buy food or anything else I might need along the way. Bernie was afraid that it wouldn't be enough, but I wasn't worried. If I needed money, I was sure I could find a way to get some.

I was hungry, but I didn't want to waste money on the food in the bus station, so when I got back on the bus, I ate one of the ham sandwiches Bernie had packed, and afterward a package of Zander's chocolate Devil Dogs. The food stopped my stomach from growling, but I still had that uncomfortable hollow feeling deep down inside. Alice woke up from her nap refreshed and feeling talkative again. She was more of a teller than an asker, but I didn't mind. Her chatter helped keep my mind off other things.

She talked on and on into the night about the reunion in Salt Lake. One way or another, fifty-two Wilinskys were making their way there. Her clan, she called them. Some, she explained, she got along with "famously" and others she could have "done without."

When she started talking about the feud she was having with her sister, Ellen, over who had given better Christmas presents the year before, I got sleepy. In fact, I fell so sound asleep, I slept right through the stop in Lovelock. It was the first time in my life Bernie and I hadn't said good night to each other.

I slept straight through till the next morning. When I woke up, my neck was stiff and the kittens were making a pitiful racket under the seat. Alice put her finger to her lips and then, making sure the driver didn't see, she took them out of the bag one by one, handing two of them to me to hide under my sweater, where they settled right down.

"Do you have a big family, Heidi?" Alice asked me.

I waited without answering. I'd learned that Alice had a way of asking questions that she didn't really mean for you to answer. Besides, I didn't feel like telling Alice about my family. Listening to her go on and on about the ins and outs of her own family had begun to make me feel even more acutely aware of all the things I didn't know about mine. Alice looked at me expectantly. Apparently this time she did want an answer.

"There's Mama and Bernie and me," I said. "And I've got a grammy, too."

It felt strangely exciting to come right out and say I had a grandmother like that even though I didn't know it yet for sure. Alice didn't question it, though. Why would she? Fifty-two Wilinskys were gathering in Salt Lake City; it probably seemed only fair for me to have one measly grandmother.

"My grammy gave me this sweater as a going-away present," I added boldly.

When I'd lied to Bernie about going to buy my ticket, I had felt guilty the whole time. This was different. Easy. And I didn't feel guilty, more like giddy. Alice didn't know me. I could tell her anything I wanted to about me or my family, and she wouldn't know if I was making it up or not.

"My grammy lives with us and she gives me presents all the time," I said. "Hundreds of them."

"Mine taught me how to make pie," Alice said, turning the conversation away from me and back to herself. "The secret is in the lard. People turn their noses up at lard these days, but it's the only way to guarantee a flaky crust. Tell you what, Heidi," she said as she got up and carefully pulled a shopping bag down from the overhead baggage compartment. "I was going to bring this to the reunion, but Lord knows with all the jouncing around it'll be the worse for wear by the time I get there. How would you like to sample my strawberry rhubarb right here and now?" She pulled an aluminum pie tin out of the bag. "Who says pie's not for breakfast?"

I was hungry and I had never tasted home-made pie in my life. Bernadette wasn't a baker. She wasn't a fryer or a broiler, either. She made decent scrambled eggs, but other than that and coffee and Jell-O, I don't remember her making anything much from scratch. We ate mostly frozen or canned things heated up. Alice's pie had little strips of dough woven like a basket across the top, and the edges were pinched up in perfect, even little waves all the way around. It was beautiful.

"My grandmother was in the 4-H," she explained as she watched me lift a forkful of pie into my mouth. "She won ribbons for her pies, and she passed on all her secrets to me because I'm her favorite grandchild."

I didn't know the first thing about baking pies, but for reasons I couldn't understand, all of a sudden those secrets Alice's grandmother had passed on to her made me so jealous it hurt.

"My grammy bakes too," I said. "She's the best baker in the world. But she doesn't bake pies. Just cakes—the kind with lots of layers with frosting in between and pink roses on top. We're big cake eaters in my family. All of us."

As I talked, I ate pie. Bite after bite, unable to stop myself, just like the lying.

"Cake, cake, cake, that's all anybody ever

thinks about at my house," I said through a mouthful of pie.

Alice watched as I boll-weeviled my way through that whole pie. When I finally pressed my fork down on the last bite in the bottom of the tin pie plate, she smiled and said proudly, "Did you ever taste a flakier crust, Heidi?"

I shook my head and licked the fork clean. I felt sick.

The kittens under my sweater had grown restless, and their little claws were catching at the stitches in my sweater as they squirmed, so I took them out and put them back in the bag. Alice had a thermos of milk with her; she poured some in a little dish and put it in the bag for them. I was thirsty and wished she would offer me some too, but she'd brought it for the kittens, so I kept quiet.

"When's your birthday?" Alice asked me once she had resettled in her seat. This time she didn't wait for an answer. "Mine's October second," she said. Then, ticking off on her fingers, she continued, "My mother's is October tenth, my sister's is the thirteenth, my brother's is the eighteenth, and Daddy's is the twenty-seventh. We're all five of us October Wilinskys."

October Wilinskys. I felt another jealous pang. I looked at Alice and wondered—would she understand if I told her about my birthday? Did she know anyone else who had to guess about when they were born? How could an October Wilinsky possibly understand about that?

"Who named you Alice?" I asked, and braced myself for another pang because I was sure she would know.

"It's a Wilinsky tradition," she began. "The name Alice has been in the family for generations. There are scads of us. My grandmother and my great-grandmother on my father's side were Alices, and there are two uncles who married Alices, and gosh, there must be at least three other Alices I can't think of right now."

The thought of all those Wilinskys, running around happily naming their babies after each other, made me antsy, and again I felt driven to bend the truth like a soft twig.

"I was named after the movie," I told her.

"The one with Shirley Temple in it."

"Really? Oh, I love Shirley Temple," Alice said, clasping her hands together with delight. "All those wonderful curls, and that cute little pout. I'm a big fan."

"My grammy knows her," I went on, trying my best to make it sound like that was no big deal, just one of many interesting things about me.

"She *knows* Shirley Temple? You mean personally?" Alice asked.

My chest swelled with pride. I was discovering something else about lying. When people believe what you say, sometimes you forget you're not telling the truth.

"Shirley Temple's the one who taught my grammy how to bake cakes. She's a very good baker," I said.

Alice looked at me for a minute.

"*The* Shirley Temple we're talking about? The movie star? She taught your grandmother how to bake?" she said.

I nodded.

"She comes over and bakes at our house all the time," I said.

"Shirley Temple comes to your house?" Alice said.

"Yes. She says she likes our oven better than hers," I said.

"I see," Alice said, nodding and pulling a loose thread on her sleeve. "You must have a very nice oven at your house."

"Yep," I said. "Shirley Temple comes over all the time to use it, and after she and my grammy bake cakes, they decorate them and stick candles in them, and then we all sit around together and pretend it's somebody's birthday."

"And she comes over to do this pretty often, does she? Bake cake in your oven?" asked Alice.

"Very often," I said. "All the time, really. Except of course when she's busy in Hollywood making movies."

"Of course," she said. "Tell me something, Heidi—when Shirley Temple comes over to bake with your grammy, does she ever tap-dance for you, show you the steps she's working on for her next movie maybe?"

"Sometimes she does," I said. "Sometimes she dances."

"In your kitchen?" asked Alice.

"Or in the living room," I said.

"And does she sing sometimes too?" Alice asked.

"Sometimes," I told her. "If she's in the mood."

Alice laughed. Then she looked down at her lap and didn't say anything for a minute, and I knew something was wrong.

"Heidi," she finally said, "like I told you, I'm a big Shirley Temple fan. I think I've seen every one of her movies at least a dozen times, which is why I happen to know she hasn't made a new one since *A Kiss for Corliss*, back in the late 1940s. She's an old lady now, almost eighty years old. Into politics. A staunch Republican. She doesn't tap-dance in your kitchen any more than I do."

"Oh," I said, or tried to anyway. My lips could only manage to form around the sad roundness of the word; no sound actually came out. Now I understood. She'd known all along that I was lying. About the dancing and singing and the baking. About everything. She'd listened to me and kept me going just the way I did with Zander, nodding and uh-huhing and egging me on, all the while knowing that I was making it up.

Why had she done that? Why hadn't she told me she knew I was lying? Maybe for the same reason I didn't tell Zander. She was more interested in trying to figure out for herself what lay underneath the lies. But I wasn't like Zander—I wasn't lying because the truth was too hard to admit. I wasn't hiding the truth. If that's what she wanted, I would just give it to her.

"I don't have a birthday," I said. "And my mama's got a bum brain and I'm not sure if I have a grammy or not."

She didn't say anything.

"Bernie says it's like Mama and I dropped from the sky," I told her.

"Hmm." Alice nodded and brushed a cat hair from her skirt, but she didn't ask me to explain. She was an October Wilinsky. She had a grandmother who shared her name and told her secrets and loved her best of all. She didn't need to know the truth about me. She didn't even want to.

The air between us was thick and uncomfortable to breathe after that. Alice read magazines, licking her fingertip each time she turned the page. The kittens cried, but she didn't offer to let me hold them. When we finally reached Salt Lake City, Alice tucked the magazines back in her bag, put on lipstick, and combed her hair.

"You take good care now, Heidi," she said as she slipped into her long green raincoat.

When she'd come and sat down next to me in the Reno bus station wearing that coat, I'd felt as though I'd been found, but as she stepped off the bus and I heard the kittens mewing and Alice clicking her tongue to comfort them, I was sure that I had never felt more lost in my life.

CHAPTER ELEVEN

Good

I called Bernie from a phone inside the Salt Lake City station. She was drinking her morning cup of coffee.

"I'm sorry I didn't call you last night, Bernie. I slept through Lovelock," I told her.

"I figured as much, but it didn't stop me any from worrying," she said. "How are you, baby?"

How was I supposed to answer that? After what I'd just been through with Alice, I wanted to tell Bernie the truth. But if she knew I was sad and homesick, she would tell me to turn around and come back. I wasn't sure I would be able to say no—and what bothered me even more was that I wasn't sure I remembered why I was supposed to.

A large red-faced man stopped right in

front of me to light up a thick black cigar. He puffed on it a few times, then puckered his lips and blew out the match. A soft familiar sound passed through the air to me on a stream of gray smoke—*soof*—and I remembered.

"You okay?" Bernie said.

"Yes, Bernie," I said. "I'm fine."

The line crackled.

"Oooh! Did you hear that?" she said.

"What was it?"

"Thunder boomers. It's pouring buckets here today," she said. "You know how your mama feels about rain. She's been hiding under the covers since it started."

More crackle, then the line hissed and cleared.

"Are you still there, Bernie? Bernie?"

"Calm down, baby. I'm right here," she said. "And I'm putting a red pushpin right smack dab on Salt Lake City so I know exactly where you are the way I always—"

The line crackled again, hissed, and this time, when it cleared, she wasn't there anymore.

"Bernie? *Bernie?*" I shouted into the phone.

I stood there for a while with the phone pressed tight against my ear, but she didn't come back. There wasn't time to call her again. As it was, I had to run to make it back to the bus in time. Luckily the driver wasn't paying attention, or maybe he just didn't care that Alice wasn't with me anymore.

I found a new seat and sat by myself, sleeping on and off until we got to our next stop, Rock Springs, Wyoming. We switched drivers there, but not buses, so even though I desperately wanted to hear Bernie's voice, I decided I had to play it safe and stay on the bus. I didn't know if the new driver would have the same feeling about me traveling alone, and I just didn't feel up to facing having to find someone new to get me back on. I ate the second ham sandwich, taking tiny bites to make it last as long as possible. Then I did the same with the last package of Devil Dogs.

The conversation with Alice played over and over in my head. I wished I had a mental switch to turn it off. I kept trying to convince myself that it didn't matter what she thought of me since we'd never in a million years cross paths again. I couldn't help but wonder, though, if she was standing around with a bunch of other Alices at that very moment laughing about the silly kid on the bus who'd told her that Shirley Temple had tap-danced in her kitchen. It was humiliating to think about, but it wasn't what was really bothering me.

What bothered me was not knowing why I'd done it. A lie is the opposite of the truth. Truth is good and lies are bad. Black and white. Simple. Still, I'd lied to Alice for no good reason, and I hadn't even felt bad about it until I'd gotten caught. What did that say about me?

I got out my notebook and started a new list:

Things I Know About Lying

Lying is bad
Lying is wrong
Sometimes people lie because the
   truth is too hard to admit
Sometimes it's easy to do

Sometimes if you're not careful you
    start to believe your own lies
Sometimes it makes you feel guilty
Sometimes it doesn't
People don't always tell you when they
    know you're lying

By the time we reached our next stop,
Cheyenne, I was sick. My stomach had gone
from hollow to hurting and I was worried that I
might need to throw up. Bernie always brought
me a bowl and held my forehead for me when I
threw up. And afterward she gave me a stick of
Doublemint gum to get rid of the taste.

I was the first one off the bus and I didn't
care if it meant having to find somebody to
help me get back on. Maybe I wouldn't get back
on. Maybe I would call Bernie and tell her I
was sick and she would make me come home.
Make me give up. And maybe I would go home.
Home to Mama and Bernie.

I found a phone booth and dialed the
number, but instead of an operator I got
a recording saying that they were unable to
complete the call at that time. I tried twice

more, but still got the recording. I was half doubled over from the pain in my stomach. Through the window of the booth I saw a little shop near the ladies' room and decided to go buy a package of Doublemint just in case, but when I got there I changed my mind and asked for a cup of black coffee instead. The woman seemed surprised, and for a second I thought maybe she wasn't going to sell it to me.

But I handed her a dollar and she handed me my change and a blue-and-white cardboard cup with a plastic lid. I took a quick sip. It was even more bitter than Bernie's coffee, but I didn't care—I wasn't going to drink it. I was only going to hold it and smell it and let it lead me back where I wanted to be—in the kitchen with Bernie grinding beans in her bathrobe while Mama colored in the living room.

The phone booths in Cheyenne were the nice kind with little seats and a light that went on when you pulled the glass door shut. I found an empty one, went in, and closed the door. The familiar smell of the coffee quickly filled the small space, making it almost cozy, and I began to feel a little better. I set the cup of coffee on the metal shelf beneath the phone and dialed Bernie's number once more. This time an operator came on the line.

"Collect call from Heidi," I said, relieved to hear a human voice.

"Sorry, Hon, they've got weather out there and the lines are down," she told me.

"Down? For how long?" I asked.

"Hard to say," she told me. "Couple of hours, couple of days. Depends on what the problem is."

A couple of days? If I got back on the bus, in a couple of days I would be in Liberty.

"Can you try it again, please?" I asked. "It's important."

"Sure can, but it's not going to change anything. Like I said, the lines are down, and down is down."

I tried Bernie unsuccessfully several more times until finally I heard them make the announcement for my bus. The coffee had grown cold in the cup and the smell was working a darker kind of magic now. Panic had set in, and I felt sicker even than before. Bernie's voice was the only thing I knew that could possibly fill the hollow space that had finally taken over and was about to turn me inside out.

I hung up the phone with shaky hands and slid open the glass door. *Soof*, it whispered as it folded back on itself to let me through. I clamped my hands over my ears. I didn't want to hear it. Not now. I didn't want to be reminded. I didn't want anything except to get to a trash can. I was going to be sick.

The overhead light had clicked off when I opened the door, and I stood in the shadows, shivering as a powerful wave of nausea washed over me. I could see the trash can, only a few feet away, but I couldn't seem to move. I closed my eyes and tried to make myself step out of the booth, but I was frozen in place. Then a faraway voice came to me—at first I thought it was Bernie's, a talking memory in my head; then I realized it was my own voice I was hearing. I was talking out loud to myself, the sound distorted and echoey because my hands were still covering my ears—

"Round the block, up, down, curl the tail onto the next. Round the block, up, down, curl the tail onto the next."

I stumbled out of the booth and made a mad dash for the trash can, reaching it just in the nick of time. Three times I retched and gagged into the big blue metal can, and when at last it was finally over, I opened my eyes and blinked. There was Georgia Sweet.

"Doublemint?" she asked, holding out the pack to me.

She was tall and thin, and that day we met Georgia had on a long yellow dress with blue flowers on it. She told me she was eighteen years old and had lived in Wheatland, Wyoming, her whole life, but that she was on her way to New York City, to go to college. New York City is a long way from Wheatland, Wyoming, but it's only two and a half hours from Liberty. We would be riding on the same bus for the next two days. Once again I had been found.

"How did you know about the Doublemint?" I asked her as we showed our tickets and got on the bus together.

Georgia had insisted on buying me a Coke to help settle my stomach, and I was feeling much better.

"My mom always gave me Doublemint after an urp," she said. "Yours too?"

"My mother has a bum brain, so she doesn't really take care of me. Bernie is the one who gives me gum," I said, determined to get off on a truthful first step with Georgia.

"Is Bernie your dad?" she asked,

"No. She's my neighbor, but she sort of lives with us. She's family. There are just the three of us, plus maybe I have a grandmother but I don't know for sure yet. It's kind of a long story," I said.

Georgia was the opposite of Alice. She was an asker, not a teller. I answered a million questions during the two days Georgia and I traveled together. Like I'd told her, mine was a long story, but apparently Georgia wanted to hear it, and I guess I wanted to tell it because I didn't hold much of anything back.

"Want a Violet?" Georgia asked at one point during a lull in the conversation. She rummaged in her purse, then held out a roll of candies wrapped in silver foil.

I took a candy but spit it out after only a second.

"Tastes like perfume," I said.

"Uh-huh. Makes your breath fresh, see?" She blew a little stream of warm flowery air in my direction.

"Yep," I said.

"It's very important to have good breath," she said.

I wanted to ask her if mine was okay, but I felt too shy. Instead I slipped the Violet back in my mouth and sucked on it just in case.

"Do you think you'll go to college when you get out of high school?" Georgia asked me.

I hadn't told her yet about me not going to school.

"Bernie teaches me," I said, "so I won't go to high school. I guess she'll teach me college, too."

"I don't think one person can teach college—it takes tons of professors to do it," Georgia said. "Besides, what if you want to study something Bernie doesn't know about?"

"Like what?" I asked.

"I don't know. Like home ec. That's what my mom majored in at college," Georgia said.

"What's home ec?" I asked.

"Home economics. Back then they taught

that kind of stuff to women, you know, cooking and sewing and how to be a perfect mother."

"Is she a perfect mother?" I asked.

"Well, I guess she *was,* but I don't really remember because she got cancer and died when I was five."

I didn't know what to say. Nobody I knew had ever died. Except for Bernie's father—and I didn't know him, I just knew about him. I felt really bad for Georgia—I couldn't imagine how it would feel to lose Mama or Bernie.

"I'm sorry," I said. "I didn't know."

"How could you? It's not like it shows on a person, what they don't have," she said.

Georgia was eighteen years old and on her way to college. She knew who her mother and father were and that they had chosen her name because her mother had been born in Atlanta. She had two sets of grandparents and a dog named Frisky who was allowed to sleep on her bed. But in spite of all that was different, in some deep, important way Georgia and I were like the two yellow ducks in the Memory game, one in the middle and one in the upper left-hand corner—matching.

"Do you miss her?" I asked.

"Not really. My dad is great, and since I've only really ever had him, it just feels normal, know what I mean?" she said.

Y.D. Yellow ducks. I knew exactly what she meant. You can't miss what you don't remember ever having.

"Have you ever heard of the word *soof*?" I asked.

"Spell it," she said.

I did, but she shook her head. That's when I told her about Mama's list and how that word had been the reason I'd left Reno in the first place.

"Do you think *soof* is a person?" she asked.

"I don't know," I said. "Maybe."

"Has your mother always been the way she is, or did something happen to her to make her that way?" Georgia asked.

"I think always, but I don't know for sure," I answered.

"What about your dad—did he have a bum brain too?"

"I don't know who my dad was," I said.

"Maybe he's *soof*," she said.

I had begun to think that certain things that seem to happen by accident don't really happen by accident at all. Like luck, but even more mysterious. If I hadn't met Alice and made myself sick over all that lying, and if the phone line had been working instead of down, maybe I wouldn't have ever met Georgia. And if I hadn't met Georgia, I wouldn't have told her all the things I told her and she wouldn't have thought to wonder if *soof* was something it hadn't even occurred to me it might be. My father's name.

CHAPTER TWELVE

Again

"Are you going to study home ec at college, like your mom did?" I asked Georgia.

"No, I'm going to major in psych," she said.

"What's that?"

"Psychology. What makes people tick." She tapped her temple twice with her long pointer finger. I loved to watch Georgia's hands. They were graceful and pale, and when she talked, they moved around her like birds flying. "I either want to be a social worker or maybe a shrink."

"What *does* make people tick?" I asked.

"Lots of things. A brain is like a watch. Did you ever see inside a watch or an old clock?"

I shook my head.

"My dad showed me once. There are all these moving parts. Gears and cogs and screws and springs, and they all have to work together perfectly or it won't keep time right."

I thought about Bernie saying Mama was like a machine with broken parts. I'd always pictured a washing machine for some reason, but now I imagined Mama with a clock inside her head, one that didn't keep time.

"Do you think there's any way to fix somebody's brain if it's not working right?" I asked.

"Sometimes," she said.

"How?" I asked.

"You can see a shrink," she said.

"What do they do?" I asked.

"Ask questions. Talk about your dreams. I took psychology as my senior elective last year, but truthfully, I don't remember a lot of it that well. Except the stuff about body language. I think that's just so fascinating," she said.

"What's body language?" I asked her.

"Well, like, see that guy over there, three seats up in the red shirt? See how he's leaning away from the woman who's talking to him? He doesn't like talking to her, and even though he's not telling her that with words, he's telling her that with his body. That's body language."

I looked at the man and saw that he was kind of leaning away from the woman sitting next to him.

"Maybe she has bad breath," I said.

Georgia giggled. I liked that I'd made her laugh. "Maybe you should give her a Violet," I added.

She laughed again.

"Know what this means?" Georgia asked me as she intertwined her fingers and put her arms behind her head.

I shook my head.

"It means you're a confident person," she said.

"How come?" I asked.

"I'm not sure—they just say it does. And they also say if you touch your face a lot, especially your lips, when you're talking to someone, it means you're attracted to them. Also most people do something weird and obvious when they're lying. Twitch or blink or cough or something. It's called a tell."

"Really? Do I have a tell?" I asked.

"I don't know. Tell me a lie and I'll tell you if you do," she said, looking closely at my face.

"Shirley Temple taught my grandmother how to bake," I said.

"*Really*?" said Georgia, her eyes going wide.

"No, you said I should lie so you could see if I do anything weird," I said.

"Oh, I forgot to look, I got so interested in your story. I love Shirley Temple movies. Try again."

"Shirley Temple taught my grandmother how to bake," I said, looking Georgia right in the eye.

"Well, I didn't see anything weird, but maybe that's just because you told it twice, so you got used to it or something."

I didn't tell her I'd actually told that lie three times.

Later I would add two things to my "Things I Know About Lying" list—

The more times you tell a lie, the
    harder it gets to tell you're lying
Liars have tells

I tried Bernie at every stop we made after Cheyenne, but the lines stayed down. I was worried, but I was sure that Bernie was even more worried than me. I knew she was at home in Reno with Mama, but for the first time ever, Bernie didn't know where I was. *Fly under the radar*, she had said to me all those times, but now I was out there without any radar to fly under.

I showed Georgia the photographs of Hilltop and told her all the things I hoped to find out, and she never once made me feel like I was crazy to want to *know*.

"I'd be just like you," she said. "I'd want to know everything. I'd have to."

Y.D.

"I've always been like that," she went on. "Haven't you noticed how many questions I ask? My father says I'm one of those people who leave no stone unturned."

Before I'd left Reno, it had seemed to me that the whole world was filled with people who knew exactly who they were, where they were going, and why they were doing what they were doing. I saw them everywhere I went. Walking down the street, standing on corners waiting to cross, mailing letters. People who knew. Georgia was one of those people too. She knew all those important things about herself that I wanted to know. The difference was, unlike those other people, the ones I envied and maybe even hated a little bit for knowing, I was happy for Georgia. I was glad that she knew.

At every stop Georgia and I got off and on together. The stations blended together after a while. Each time I would try Bernie, and each time Georgia would reassure me that eventually the lines would be back up.

"Just think how happy she'll be to hear your voice when you finally do get through," she said.

I had told Georgia about my lucky streak, of course, since I was telling her everything, but there were no slot machines around for me to prove it to her. It's not that she didn't believe me—she said she did—but I still wanted to show her. Finally in a bus station in Des Moines, I figured out a way to do it.

"Stand over here and don't say anything," I told her. "Just watch."

I looked around the station for a minute

until found what I was looking for, sitting on a bench near the rest rooms, then I headed over to the newsstand.

"Two Quickscratch lottery tickets, please," I said.

"Little young for gambling, ain't you, half-pint?" the man said. "I can't sell you tickets, you know."

"Oh, these aren't for me, sir. My mother asked me to do it for her. She says I'm luckier than her. She's over there on the bench near the door. See?" I pointed to a woman sitting on a far-off bench by the rest rooms, busily digging around in her handbag.

"It's okay for you to sell me tickets, so long as I've got an adult with me, right? She's with me; she's just over there looking for her glasses. She always loses them," I said. "I tell her she should get one of those chains to hang them around her neck, but she always forgets to do it. Mama! Yoo-hoo! Mama!" I called over in her direction.

The woman kept pawing through her bag and didn't look up when I called.

"She can't hear when she's not wearing her

glasses," I explained (something Bernie had once pointed out had been true of her father). "Isn't that weird?"

"Uh-huh. Okay," he said, taking a last look at the woman on the bench before handing me two tickets.

I paid him and then used my fingernail to scratch off the silver squares over the numbers on the tickets. I won seven bucks on the first one and three on the second. He looked a little surprised.

"Look, Mama!" I called out as I waved the ten-dollar bill he handed me in the air. "We won!"

Georgia was very impressed. I treated us both to hamburgers, milk shakes, and fries with the ten dollars I won. I knew that Bernie considered that junk food, but I had a feeling she would forgive me. For the first time since I'd left Reno, I actually felt full.

"Do you think I'll make a good shrink?" Georgia asked me as we pulled out of Des Moines and got back on the highway. "Frank says he thinks I'm too high-strung for it."

I pictured a clothesline hanging way up high with long johns and nightgowns and Georgia hung up by the shoulders with clothespins, her long skinny legs swinging back and forth in the breeze.

"Who's Frank?" I asked.

"Frank Gregory. He's just a boy I like," she said.

I had one of my jealous pangs.

"Frank is wrong. You'll be a perfect shrink," I told her.

We talked awhile longer, and then Georgia dozed off.

I took out my notebook and turned to a blank page to start a new list I'd been thinking about making.

Things I Know About Georgia Sweet

birthday: August 12
middle name: Elizabeth (named after
     her grandmother)
father's name: John Albert Sweet
     high school math teacher
     likes fishing

mother's name: Louise Ann Sweet
    born in Atlanta
    majored in home ec
    died of cancer when Georgia was five
dog's name: Frisky
    sleeps on the bed
    likes M&M's and cheese
other pets: none
    (would like to have a monkey
        someday or a talking parrot)
likes: fresh breath, strawberry milk
    shakes, ketchup on French fries,
    the color yellow, psychology, body
    language, Doublemint gum, Violets,
    Frisky, old movies, fishing with her
    dad, asking questions

dislikes: sleeping sitting up, flying
    on airplanes, mayonnaise

wants: to be a shrink
        to know everything
secret: likes a boy named Frank
    Gregory

I left a lot of extra space after *likes* and *dislikes*, because I knew the more Georgia and I talked, the more there would be to add to the list. I wished she would wake up so that I could find out what her favorite book was, and whether she liked Devil Dogs as much as I did. She stirred and I turned to look at her. The notebook fell off my lap, and when I leaned down to pick it up off the floor, it had flopped open to a page near the front of the book, to an old list with only one entry under the heading.

Things I Know About Mama

Name: So B. It

How was it that I knew so much more about Georgia, a person I had only known for a day, than I did about my own mother? Bernie had told me to find someone who could be my mother. Someone who was safe. Sitting there beside Georgia, seeing her long arms crossed over her chest as she slept, I knew I had found the right person, but was she like a mother? And when I really thought about it, was Mama?

On the fourth day of my trip we reached New York City. I was excited. I knew I was almost there, almost to Liberty. But I was scared. I had not spoken to Bernie since Wyoming, and now I would be losing Georgia, too. I wished she was coming with me.

"I hope you find *soof*," Georgia told me as we got off the bus. "And your grammy. And everything."

Georgia didn't have to catch another bus, so she walked with me through the giant station, up the escalators and over to the ShortLine gates, where I would catch my bus to Liberty. The Port Authority bus station was very crowded compared to everywhere else we'd stopped. There were stores and sit-down restaurants and even a bowling alley. I had tried Bernie from a phone booth but with no luck. Georgia stopped to buy a package of Violets at the newsstand. While she stood in line to pay, I wandered over to watch a Japanese man who was sitting on a stool playing beautiful, sad music on an instrument with one long string. As I stood there listening, I felt a sharp tug on my knapsack, but when I turned around nobody was there.

At the gate Georgia helped me choose my next "mother," a friendly woman named DeeDee Monroe. I got her chatting about the weather without much effort, and as we got on together, I turned and waved a last good-bye to Georgia.

"Who's that?" DeeDee asked me.

"My sister," I told her, and this time I knew I was lying because the truth was too hard to admit. A sister is someone you will always know, no matter what happens.

"Oh sure 'nuf," she said. "I can see the resemblance."

It was a gray day and it was dark on the bus. I turned on the little light over my seat, which sent a focused beam of buttery glow down into my lap. I opened the front pocket of my backpack, took out the packet of photos from Hilltop, and went through them one by one. All the faces were familiar by now. Strangers and at the same time not. When I came to the picture I'd torn in half, which

Bernie and I had later taped back together, I stopped. I set it on the top of the stack and stared at it for a while. Then I closed my eyes and tried to picture the smiling blond woman in the red sweater.

"Hello, Grammy," I said out loud.

And I imagined her voice answering me, clear and bright and strong—

"Hello, Heidi. What on earth took you so long?"

CHAPTER THIRTEEN

Blue

The bus to Liberty took a total of two and a half hours, which meant I would get there around three o'clock in the afternoon. I sat very still in my seat the whole time, as though moving around might cause the fear inside me to spark and ignite. I imagined a huge hand pressing down on my anxiety, keeping it inside like the springy clown head of a jack-in-the-box.

DeeDee didn't seem to mind my being quiet. She was busy knitting a long scarf for her nephew, who lived up in Albany where, she told me, winters are so cold thoughts freeze solid in your brain before you even have time to think them.

We made only one stop between New York City and Liberty. Monticello, where I would change buses for the last time. I was hungry, so I found a stand selling hot pretzels and lemonade, waited in line, and ordered two pretzels and a small drink. When I went to pay, I discovered that the little side pocket of my knapsack was empty. My money was gone.

I found a phone and tried Bernie once more.

"Please," I whispered, "please be there."

But the call did not go through.

I felt panicky and sick to my stomach again. Bernie and Mama and Georgia—all gone, and now my luck had deserted me too. Why hadn't I listened to Bernie when she had said to wait until I was older?

There was nothing to do but to get back on the bus and hope that somehow something would happen between there and Liberty to change things. I gathered what wits I had left and chose a new "mother," Nancy. She was carrying a thick book with a bookmark stuck in about halfway through and she wore glasses on a chain around her neck. She didn't say much as we got on the bus together, but she had a batch of homemade chocolate chip cookies with her that she shared with me once we sat down. I ate one, but my stomach was too queasy to handle more. What would I do if I reached Liberty and still couldn't get through to Bernie? It seemed as though my luck had disappeared right out from under me when I needed it most. I thought about asking Nancy for money, but somehow I couldn't bring myself to do it. I wanted Bernie. I wanted to be myself again. Lucky and happy and home.

Twenty minutes later the driver announced—

"Liberty! This stop is Liberty!"

My hands were shaking and my heart pounded in my throat as I stepped off the bus. As I pulled my little suitcase out of the baggage compartment and set it down on the sidewalk, it began to rain. The driver hitched up his pants and, without looking back, climbed on board. The door swung closed and he drove off, turning the corner and disappearing from sight.

The Liberty bus stop was no more than a bent metal signpost sticking out of a cracked square of rough sidewalk. There was no building or shelter. Within a minute everyone else who had gotten off the bus was gone, picked up by smiling people who had been standing there waiting for them. As I stood alone on the main street of Liberty, New York, the wind blew right through me like I wasn't even there. Faded American flags hung from the street-lamps along with torn bits of tinsel garland left over from old Christmas decorations.

There was a grimy pay phone bolted to the wall of a grocery store with boarded-up windows. I called Bernadette. I wasn't hopeful, but I didn't know what else to do.

"Collect call from Heidi," I said softly.

And this time the call went through.

"Heidi! Oh thank God, Heidi." Bernie started crying. "Where are you? Are you okay? I've been scared out of my wits," she sobbed. "Oh, Heidi. Heidi."

I knew I should tell her that I was fine, and that I had made it to Liberty in one piece, but the moment I heard her voice, I fell apart. The knot that had begun to form in my stomach way back in Cheyenne when the lines had first gone down, and had turned knuckle-white hard after I'd discovered my money had been stolen, began to uncurl, and as it loosened, everything I had been holding back rushed to the surface. I stood there with my little suitcase clamped between my legs, bawling into the phone. I came completely unglued—no words, just sobs, and on the other end Bernadette was crying and at the same time trying to soothe me with her sounds.

"Baby, baby, shh-shh-shh . . ."

I clutched the phone, weeping inconsolably.

"Heidi," Bernadette said when at last we'd both managed to calm down a little, "has somebody hurt you? Are you hurt, baby?"

"No, Bernie. Nobody hurt me, but—"

More tears.

"Tell me what's the matter, Heidi," Bernadette said. "Tell me what's happened."

I sniffed and coughed and sniffed again.

"Nothing's happened. I'm here, Bernie. I'm in Liberty. But it's not how I thought it would be. It's all *different*."

"Different how?" she asked.

"Like something's ending instead of beginning," I said.

"What do you mean?" she asked.

"On the bus I felt like I was going some-where. But now that I'm here, it feels like I'm nowhere. Nobody even knows I'm here."

"That's not true, Heidi. I know you're there," Bernie said. "Thank God I know where you are again. And I'm looking at the exact spot on the map where you're standing right now. Li-ber-ty. Why, I can practically see you. In fact, I'm waving at you. Don't you see me? I'm the worried one in the pink housecoat who hasn't slept in two nights."

I laughed a little—I couldn't help myself. It was so good to have her back.

"That's my girl," Bernie said. "You have no idea how frantic I've been about you, baby, but without a phone I couldn't even call the police. I don't want to tell you the horrible things I imagined. Oh God, Heidi, if anybody has hurt you, I'll never forgive myself."

"Nobody hurt me, Bernie. But somebody stole all my money. I don't have the cab fare anymore."

"We'll fix that. It's not important," she said. "Don't you worry, baby. I can get money to you somehow."

I heard Mama in the background calling for Bernie. She sounded upset. More than just rimply.

"What's wrong with Mama?" I asked.

"She's been having a time of it, poor thing," Bernie said.

"What kind of a time?" I asked, suddenly on edge. "Mama's okay, isn't she?"

"Yes, baby, but her headaches have been really bad," Bernie said.

Mama was yelling now.

"Dette! Dette!"

"I'm sorry," Bernadette said. "I don't know what to do. I should go to her before she hurts herself. She needs me, Heidi."

"I need you too," I whispered. But Mama was yelling louder by then and I don't think Bernie heard what I said.

"Call me back in ten minutes," she said. "I'll try to calm her down. We'll talk about the money and figure something out," she told me. "I've got to go now. I'm sorry."

"What if I can't reach you again?" I said anxiously, but she was already gone.

I hung up the phone and wiped my nose on

the rolled-up sleeve of my red sweater. It no longer smelled of Bernie and home. I wanted to stand there and wait the ten minutes before calling her back, but what had begun as a light drizzle was fast becoming a rainstorm. My jeans were soaked through already, sticking to my skin, and my hair was dripping wet. It was much colder here than it had been in Reno. I looked around but didn't see the taxi place anywhere, and there was nobody out on the street to ask. The town seemed deserted. Empty. There was a flash of lightning and a loud thunderclap. I shivered and pulled my hands up inside my sleeves. Seeing a little magazine store with a light on across the street, I picked up my suitcase and hurried across to it.

The man behind the counter was reading a paper. He looked up when I came in, pushed his glasses up onto his bald head, and waited.

"Can you tell me where ABC Cab is?" I asked.

"Two doors down," he grunted, nodding his head just hard enough to knock his glasses down onto his nose.

I went back outside. Another flash of lightning split the sky, followed by a boom of thunder so loud, it rattled the windows behind me. Rain was coming down hard and fast at an angle, and I had to jump over several large puddles to get to the tiny little storefront two doors down with a faded cardboard sign in the window I hadn't noticed before. ABC CAB.

"How much to Hilltop Home?" I said, shutting the door behind me and wiping the water off my face with my wet sleeve.

"Hilltop?" the man behind the counter said, giving me a slow, long look. "I thought that place was closed down."

"It's not," I said.

"If you say so. It's quite a ways from here though. Cost you fifteen."

I knew that already, of course, but I was stalling for time. I was supposed to call Bernie back in a few minutes. Maybe if I called her from here, she would be able to talk the man into driving me up to Hilltop for free somehow. I looked around for a phone, and that was when I noticed the jelly-bean jar on the counter filled with ancient candy, faded and crackled. The sign taped to the side of the jar said, GUESS HOW MANY—WIN THE BEANS, PLUS A FREE RIDE!

"Can I hold the jar?" I asked the man.

He jerked his head toward it as a way of saying okay. "Feeling lucky?" he asked.

Was I? When I'd played the slots in Reno and bought the lottery ticket with Georgia, I hadn't *felt* lucky. Luck didn't *feel* like anything; it was just there. Like air. Then when the phone lines had gone down and I couldn't reach Bernie and my money had been stolen, I felt like my luck had deserted me. Left. I could feel its absence, like when you lose a tooth and there's an empty space there that you can't help touching with your tongue because it feels so strange.

The man watched me as I picked up the jar and turned it slowly all the way around. All the colors in the rainbow, just like Mama's shoe box full of crayons. I closed my eyes and took a deep breath. Suddenly I was home, sitting in the kitchen having "school" with Bernie. Books and papers lay on the table in front of us.

"Blue!" shouted Mama happily from the other room.

"You go, Picasso!" Bernie called out to her. Then she turned to me and smiled.

You go, Picasso!

"One thousand, five hundred twenty-seven," I said.

When I opened my eyes, the man was staring at me. "That your guess?" he asked.

I nodded, and he opened the cash register drawer and pulled a little piece of cardboard out from under the money tray. His jaw dropped. He looked at it carefully, as though he couldn't believe his own eyes, and then handed it across the counter to me. The number I'd guessed was written there in small black handwriting.

"I'll be a son of a— How in blazes did you do that?"

I smiled. Turns out my luck hadn't deserted me after all. I stood there with that big jar of jelly beans in my arms, thinking just because you can't feel something doesn't mean it's not there.

"Can you take me to Hilltop?" I asked.

The man shook his head and clucked his tongue.

"Like I said, I thought the place was closed down, but hey, it's up to you where you wanna go. You won the ride fair and square. Ha, fair—*fare*—get it? My shift's done anyways. I'll take you up myself."

The "cab," an old dented station wagon, its back bumper tied on with rope, was parked in the lot across the street near where the bus had let me off. I got in the back with my suitcase, backpack, and the jar of jelly beans. I was supposed to call Bernie back, but it was still raining hard and I decided it would be better to get up to Hilltop first and to call her from there.

"Somebody 'specting you up there, are they?" the man asked as he started up the engine and set the wipers on high speed. "'Cause this free ride ain't a round trip, just so's you know. I hope they're waiting with a big towel to dry you off with." He chuckled, looking at me in the rearview mirror.

I looked out the window and caught sight of a young girl standing in the rain, her long tangled wet hair framing a narrow, serious face. For a split second I wondered who she was and what she was doing out there all alone, and then our mouths fell open at the same time as I realized I was looking at myself reflected in the window glass. She was me, Heidi It.

CHAPTER FOURTEEN

Pretty

It looked different from the photographs. Older. The shutters had been removed and the whole place was painted dark green instead of white. Only the sign was the same: HILLTOP HOME, LIBERTY, NEW YORK.

"Here we are," said the driver, stopping at the bottom of the long dirt driveway. "You're sure it's still open?"

"I'm sure," I said. "See? There are lights on up there."

"Oh, yeah, I see. Well, I brung a fare up here once years ago, and I think I remember there's no good place to turn around up top, so since it ain't raining no more, you mind walking up?"

I said I didn't mind, thanked him, and got out.

"That was some lucky guess you made back there, kid," the driver said just before he pulled away. "Man oh man, what I'd give for a little of that kind of luck on bingo night."

I stood there looking up at the place I'd traveled all this way to get to, and it looked back down at me with half-shut window eyes and a porch mouth full of railing teeth.

Listen to the eyes, Heidi.

But I couldn't tell anything from Hilltop's face.

Even though it wasn't that far away from downtown Liberty, only about fifteen minutes or so, the storm had either skipped over the area or not reached it yet. The sky was an ominous dark gray, but the ground was still dry. As I started slowly up the steep driveway, a sudden gust of wind blew through and caught in the shaggy boughs of an old hemlock tree. *Soof*, they whispered softly as they swayed overhead. This time I didn't cover my ears. I was glad to hear Mama's word there, reminding me one more time why I had come. My shoes kicked up little clouds of fine brown dust as I quickened my pace and hurried up the driveway.

Up the wide porch steps, past a couple of pots of flowers and a pair of white-painted rocking chairs with wicker seats. The square panes of glass in the front door were covered by a lace curtain inside. I knocked but nobody answered. Setting my suitcase and the jar of jelly beans down on the porch, I knocked again, and when nobody came, I turned the knob and walked in.

It smelled old and musty, like Bernadette's medicine cabinet when you first slid it open. There wasn't much furniture in the front room, just a vinyl couch with big round buttons on the cushions and a couple of matching arm-chairs.

"Hello?" I called out, and after a minute again—"Hello?"

No answer, so I went down the hall toward the sound of the voices. I passed a large kitchen on my left with big metal pots hanging from a rack over a long counter, and on the right a bathroom with white-and-black checkered floor tiles. Then came a small room set up like an office, with a phone and a typewriter on the desk. The voices were coming from behind a tall wooden door at the end of the hall, and as I got closer, I was able to make out bits and pieces of what was being said inside. There was music playing, either a record or someone strumming a guitar.

"David, do you want to be the cheese?" I heard a woman's voice ask.

At least that's what it sounded like she'd said. I felt uncomfortable standing out in the hall like that, eavesdropping,

"Hello?" I called again, hoping maybe the woman inside would hear me, but the door was heavy, and too much was going on behind it for anyone to hear me calling. I glanced to my right, into the little office with the typewriter and phone. I hadn't noticed at first, but there was a big gray filing cabinet in there too, stuffed so full of manila folders, the drawers couldn't possibly have shut. So many folders. Hundreds. Each one tagged with a small blue label across the top that looked like it could have a name written on it.

Get whatever answers there are to be gotten, Heidi.

I wish I could say I had trouble deciding what to do next—but I didn't. I knew it was wrong, but the thought that one of those folders might contain the very truth I'd come so far to find made it easy.

Once I'd stepped inside and closed the door behind me, I found that the room was in fact considerably larger than I had originally imagined. There was a separate alcove off the little office, with a patterned rug on the floor, several plants in heavy clay pots, and a red armchair that sat with its high back toward me in front of a nice big window, overlooking a wooded hill.

Our apartment in Reno didn't get much light, so things had a hard time growing there. We tried keeping plants—ivy and jade and even an avocado we sprouted from a pit stuck round with toothpicks and hung over a jar of water—but eventually everything always died. So instead, Bernie ordered silk plants and flowers from one of her catalogues and set them in rows on the windowsills to brighten things up. Sometimes she even sprayed cologne on them.

"Wouldn't fool a bee, but it does the trick for me," she'd say as she spritzed them with the old atomizer with the faded pink squeeze ball that had belonged to her grandmother.

The plants in the alcove at Hilltop were so perfect, I wondered if they could possibly be real, especially the one that sat right next to the red armchair. It had long, slender, pointed, dark-green leaves, and off the tips of those leaves dangled strands of the prettiest flowers, so delicate and white, I just had to know for sure.

I crossed the carpet and was just about to touch one of the flowers, to rub the petals between my thumb and forefinger, when suddenly I gasped and had to clap my hand over my mouth to keep from crying out. I was not alone. There was a man sitting in the chair.

"I'm sorry. I didn't mean to bother you. I thought—I didn't think," I stammered. "There was nobody out front when I came in, so I . . ."

His face was turned away from me, and it took me a minute to realize that the reason he wasn't responding was that he was sound asleep. I heard the slow, even sound of his breathing as his chest rose and fell. I could have turned and left then, or taken a chance and done what I'd planned to do in the first place—go through the files looking for Mama. Instead, I tiptoed around to the other side of the chair in order to see his face.

His neck was bent to the side, his chin and cheek pressed down against one shoulder like a bird trying to tuck its head under a wing to sleep. His dark hair was mowed short, not much more than prickles across his scalp, and his skin was smooth and so pale, I could see blue veins pulsing in his forehead. Suddenly he shifted and stirred in his sleep, and then his head snapped up and back and he opened his eyes and looked straight at me. At first his look was blank, his jaw hanging loose, his right cheek streaked with a red imprint from the chair's upholstery. Then all of a sudden his face lit up with recognition and he broke into a wide toothy grin.

"*Sooooof* . . ." he said in a strange, soft, guttural voice, "*soooooooof* . . ."

CHAPTER FIFTEEN

Now

"Elliot? You awake? Elly?" a woman called from out in the hall. The same voice I'd heard earlier, coming from behind the big heavy door. Now she was turning the handle and coming into the room, heels clicking, crisp white pants swishing. When she saw me, she stopped short and stood with one hand on her hip, looking at me, puzzled.

"Can I help you?" she said.

I didn't answer. I couldn't. I was staring at the man in the red chair who knew Mama's word. There was something oddly familiar about him.

"Who are you?" the woman asked.

Elliot answered for me.

"*Soof*," he said, taking hold of my hand and looking over at her with the same wide grin he'd given me before.

Mama had said *soof* when she'd seen the photograph I'd torn in half, and I had wondered if *soof* was the woman in the red sweater, or maybe Mama herself. Then Georgia had made me wonder if it could be my father. Now Elliot's touch unfroze my voice just enough so that I could ask a question I hadn't thought to ask before.

"Am I *soof*?" I whispered.

Elliot smiled at me again, and the woman laughed.

"I certainly hope so. He says that word at least a hundred times a day. I'd like nothing better than to know who or what the heck he's been talking about all this time. Not even Mr. Hill seems to know," she said. "Or if he does, he won't say."

"Thurman Hill?" I asked.

She nodded.

"Elliot's father," she explained.

"But *am* I *soof*?" I asked again.

"You tell me." She laughed.

"Ruby?" I heard a man's voice calling from out in the hall.

"In here, Mr. Hill," she called back over her shoulder.

When Thurman Hill, tall and thin with a full head of thick white hair, walked into the room, I felt exactly the way I'd felt looking up at Hilltop Home for the first time from the bottom of the driveway. His face was impossible to read. Especially his eyes, which were a shade of blue I'd seen only one other place before: in the cloudy chunk of sea glass Bernie always kept in her jewelry box.

"Who are you?" he asked in a voice that sounded like it too might have been tossed about and polished smooth by a million grains of sand.

"My name is Heidi It," I said, trying hard to keep my voice from shaking, "and I have some questions I need to ask you, Mr. Hill."

"Are you a reporter for your school newspaper or something?" asked the woman he'd called Ruby. "Mr. Hill isn't much for that sort of thing, but I'd be glad to let you interview me if you'd like, though I'm boring as bread."

"I'm not from the newspaper. I just want to know if my mother used to live here," I said.

Something changed in Thurman Hill's face.

"What did you say your name was?" he asked. He bent down to get a closer look at me, and I noticed the gold watch he was wearing. The thin white hands on the blue oval face said that it was four o'clock. It had been an hour since I'd spoken to Bernie.

"Heidi It," I said.

"It? That's your last name? *I-t*?" he asked.

I nodded.

"And that's your mother's last name too, It?"

Again I nodded.

"There's never been anyone here by that name," he said, standing up straight again. "It's rather unusual. I'm sure I would remember."

"Maybe somebody else remembers," I said.

"Not very likely. This is a home for the mentally disabled. Did you know that?" he asked, not unkindly.

"My mother is mentally disabled," I said.

"That may be, but I'm afraid she wasn't here," he said. "I know everyone who's ever been here at Hilltop."

"He would. He's the big cheese," said Ruby with a wink.

"Cheese stands alone," said Elliot suddenly. "Cheese stands alone."

Ruby laughed.

"That's right, Elliot, the cheese stands alone. Good for you." Then she turned to me to explain, "It's from 'The Farmer in the Dell.' They all seem to love it for some reason. You know the song? The farmer takes a wife and the wife takes a child and all the rest, until in the end the cheese stands alone."

"What makes you think your mother was at Hilltop?" Thurman Hill asked me. "Did she tell you that?"

"No, but I've got photos," I said, reaching for my backpack.

"Wait a second. Something's ringing bells here. Are you by any chance related to somebody named Bernadette?" asked Ruby.

"Yes," I said, "she's my neighbor."

"That's the woman who's been calling from Nevada, Mr. Hill. Remember I told you about her and you said I should—"

Now there was a definite change in

Thurman Hill's face, though it would have been hard to say exactly what.

"Never mind what I said, Ruby. Is this Bernadette person with you?" he asked me, and I noticed two small red blotches had begun to form on his cheeks, just below his sharp cheekbones.

"She couldn't come," I said.

"So you're telling me you came here by yourself?" he asked. "From Nevada?"

The sea-glass eyes were sharper now, and colder, and they bored into me as he waited for my answer.

I swallowed hard and nodded.

"Did you run away?" he asked.

"No," I said.

"Shall I look up her mother in the file, Mr. Hill?" Ruby asked.

He ignored her, still staring at me intently as if I was some sort of puzzle he was trying to work out.

"May I see these photographs you say you have?" he asked quietly.

I opened my backpack and pulled out the photos, holding the stack out to him. When he reached for them, his fingers brushed against mine, and his skin was so cold that I jerked my hand away, scattering the photographs all over the floor. Ruby quickly bent and began to pick them up.

"Hey, look at this," she said, holding one of the photos out to Mr. Hill. It was the one of the people standing out on the porch under the Hilltop sign. "That's our sign, isn't it?"

"Where did you get these?" he asked, and I saw that the blotches on his cheeks were spreading like two bright red stains.

"I found the film in an old camera in a drawer," I said. "We think the pictures were taken about thirteen years ago, because Bernadette says maybe Mama was pregnant with me in the pictures and I'm twelve now."

Thurman Hill stood very still, looking at the photo in his hand, and as I watched, the color completely drained from his cheeks, until his face was absolutely powder white.

"Is this your mama here? She looks like you around the eyes," Ruby said, holding another of the photographs out to me. "And who's this other woman? She's got the same sweater on as you do. Is this your granny?"

"That's enough," Mr. Hill said sharply, and he snatched the photos away from Ruby and gave them back to me.

"What's got into you, Mr. Hill?" she asked, confused.

"Take Elliot into the room with the others, Ruby," he said.

Elliot had been sitting quietly in the chair, staring out the window at a bird that had landed in the yard.

"Come on, Elly," Ruby said. "You can have a snack. Cook has applesauce today. I know how you love applesauce."

Elliot didn't move. He was watching the bird.

"Elliot, go with Ruby, please," said Thurman Hill.

"Bird," Elliot said.

"Yes, son, that's a robin, remember?" he said gently. "You can tell by the orange breast. Now I need you to go with Ruby."

Ruby came around in front of Elliot and offered him both of her hands. Elliot took them and rose clumsily from the chair. I was surprised to see how small he was. His head didn't sit straight on his shoulders, and he held his arms in a funny way. His pants were pulled up high and fastened around his narrow waist with a leather belt, and he was barefoot.

"That's it, Elly. Come with Ruby," she said.

"Wait," I said, turning to Thurman Hill. "If my mother was never here, how does Elliot know her word? He called me *soof*."

"Ruby, take Elliot to the rec room," Thurman Hill said. "And put some socks on him, please. These floors are cold."

Ruby left then, holding Elliot by the hand like a small child.

As soon as they were gone, Thurman Hill turned to me, and this time the look on his face was easy to read. He was angry. His mouth formed a tight dark line, which cut through his face like a colorless gash halfway between his chin and his nose.

The sea-glass eyes flickered and flashed as he spoke.

"You have no right to be here," he said.

"No right?" I said. "I don't know what you're talking about."

"She's sent you here for more money, hasn't she? Well, she won't get another cent out of me. Not one. You tell her promises have been made and paid for," he answered.

His fists were balled up now like two tight white rocks.

"I don't know what you're talking about," I said. "Bernadette called and wrote, but you wouldn't answer us. That's the reason I came. I don't know anything about promises."

"*Bernadette?* Is that what she's calling herself now?" he said with a strange hollow laugh. "Well, she can call herself by any name she wants, but it doesn't change a thing. I tore up those letters and ignored her for a reason. I won't have her coming around here stirring up trouble. Not for me. Not for Elliot. Not now."

Just then a small woman in a blue dress and white sneakers pushed open the door and came running into the room.

"Come quick, Mr. H.," she said. "Elliot's having a tantrum. Ruby told me to come get you."

Her face was round like a plate, and her eyes sloped down at the corners, making her look sad even when she turned and smiled at me.

"Hello," she said. "I'm sorry to interrupt, but Mr. Hill really has to come now."

In the distance I heard what sounded like an animal howling. Thurman Hill put his hand on her shoulder and spoke gently to the woman.

"I'll be there in a minute, Sally," he said. "Go back and tell Elliot I'm coming."

"I'm afraid he's going to hurt himself," she said.

"I know. I'll be there in a minute," he said.

Then he turned back to me and his voice was hard again—

"I've done my part," he said. "Now you do yours. Leave us alone. For God's sake, just leave us alone."

Thurman Hill left me standing in the alcove feeling completely lost. I tried to make sense of the things he'd said, but I couldn't. He thought Bernadette was someone else. He thought I'd come for money. Who did he think I was? And why was he so angry?

The howling grew louder and there was a rhythmic thumping now too, like someone banging something hard against a table, or the wall.

"Elliot!" I heard Thurman Hill cry. "Don't!"

I'm not sure how long I stood there before Ruby came back in. She didn't say anything, but after a quick look over her shoulder, she pulled open one of the drawers in the gray filing cabinet and began to flip quickly through a section of folders. She went through once, and then a second time as I held my breath.

"Nothing under 'It.' Should be here if your mother was at Hilltop thirteen years ago, because these go back fifteen. But there's no 'It.'"

"Are you sure?" I asked, coming over to stand by her.

"I'm positive." She pushed against the drawer with one well-padded hip, in a vain attempt to close it. "Nothing even close. And I looked through twice. I'm sorry."

I could tell she meant it. But I just couldn't believe Mama wasn't in there somewhere. She had to be. Elliot knew her word. She was in the photographs. She'd been here. I was sure of it.

"May I look for myself?" I asked. "Just in case you missed something?"

Ruby looked nervously toward the door.

"I don't think it's a good idea," she said.

"Please." I took a step toward the filing cabinet.

"Afternoon, everybody," said a deep male voice from the doorway.

I turned around and saw an officer in a gray uniform with a wide-brimmed hat and a gold badge on his shirt. He had a gun in a black leather holster strapped around his waist.

"You ready?" he said.

Thurman Hill must have called the police and told them some lie about me being somebody I wasn't. Or maybe he'd told them I'd run away, just so they'd come and get me and he could get rid of me. I didn't know whether people got put in jail for running away or not, but I wasn't about to hang around and find out. I pushed past all of them and ran for the door as fast as I could.

CHAPTER SIXTEEN

Hot

I was halfway down the driveway, running with my backpack slung over one shoulder, the suitcase in one hand and the jelly beans under the other arm, when Sheriff Roy Franklin, Ruby's husband, finally caught up with me. He'd come to pick his wife up from work.

"Please don't take me away," I pleaded as he closed a huge hand around the top of my arm and steered me back around toward Hilltop.

"Calm down," he said. "Nobody's taking anybody anyplace. I just want to talk to you."

Ruby had come out on the front porch and was watching us walk back up the driveway. Roy carried my suitcase, and I had the jar of jelly beans in my arms. I wasn't crying, but I was close.

"Can I call Bernie?" I asked.

"Who's Bernie?" he said.

By then we'd reached the porch where Ruby was waiting, and she started to fill Roy in on my story.

"Bernie's the neighbor," she told him, "in *Nevada*. She took a bus here by herself, Roy."

"Does your family know where you are?" Roy asked.

"Yes. But Bernie's going to be worried," I told them. "I was supposed to call her back a long time ago. Please can I call her now?"

"I think maybe that's a good idea," Roy said.

We went back inside to the little office so I could call Bernie. To my relief, there was no sign of Thurman Hill anywhere.

"Oh Heidi," Bernie said as soon as the call went through, "where on earth have you been, baby? Are you all right? You were supposed to call me back ages ago."

I lost it and began to cry.

"I'm at Hilltop, Bernie. With a sheriff. Thurman Hill is awful, and he won't tell me anything. He thinks I'm somebody else. He thinks I want his money. And Mama's not in the files. I want to come home, Bernie," I sobbed into the phone. "I want to come home."

Ruby pulled a tissue out of the sleeve of her sweater and handed it to me. I blew my nose and tried to catch my breath.

"Let me speak to her," Roy said, reaching for the phone. I handed it to him and stood there sniffling and dabbing at my eyes as Ruby handed me more tissues. Roy stretched the phone cord out and moved a few feet away, then turned his back to me and kept his voice so low, I couldn't hear what he was saying to Bernadette.

My clothes were damp from the downpour I'd been caught in back in town, and I was shivering. Ruby went and made me a cup of instant hot chocolate in the kitchen, and when she came back, she brought her coat and wrapped it around my shoulders. It was warm and soft and smelled flowery, like Georgia's breath after she ate a Violet.

Roy talked to Bernadette for quite a while, and I stood there drinking my cocoa and trying not to cry again. When he was finally finished, he handed me the phone.

"I think I know the answer to this already, but tell me what his eyes are saying, baby," Bernie said. "It's important."

Sheriff Roy Franklin was a big man with black hair going gray on the sides and a large mustache that hung over both his upper and lower lip. His eyes were large and brown, dark, like the color of the ground beans in the drawer of Bernie's coffee mill. When he smiled, little lines formed at the outer corners.

"Good things," I said.

"That's what I thought," she said.

"That's one remarkable lady," Roy said after I hung up. "Wants what she wants, though."

"What did she tell you?" I asked.

He reached into his pocket. At first I thought he was going for his handcuffs and I felt a lump rise in my throat. But then he pulled out a quarter.

"Heads or tails?" he asked me.

"What?" I said.

"Heads or tails? Call it in the air," said the sheriff as he flipped the coin, caught it, and then slapped it down on the back of his other hand and covered it.

"Heads," I said.

He looked at it and nodded.

"Do it again. Heads or tails?"

"Tails," I said.

Again I was right.

He did it ten times in a row, and each time I got it right.

"What on earth, Roy?" Ruby said.

"I'll be danged, it's just like she said," said Roy.

"Like who said?" asked Ruby.

"Bernadette, the neighbor. She bet me this little girl could guess ten coin flips correctly in a row, and sure enough she did. Guess I've got no choice but to keep my part of the bargain."

"What bargain?" asked Ruby.

"I promised Bernadette that if she guessed ten flips in a row, instead of taking Heidi down to the station like I'd planned to, I'd take her to our house, feed her a home-cooked meal, and give her a warm bed to sleep in for the night."

"Roy," Ruby said.

"What, Rube? You don't want her to have to bunk downtown, do you? She's twelve years old and a couple thousand miles from home."

"Of course not," said Ruby softly. "It's just—we don't know the whole story yet."

"I know enough of it to know what's best right now. As for your boss, I need to talk to him. Where is he, anyway?"

"He's probably back in the rec room. Elly's been having a hard time this afternoon," Ruby said. "He's been banging his head."

"You meet Elliot yet?" Roy asked me.

I nodded.

"Rube's sweet on him, in case you couldn't tell," Roy said. "I'll be back in a minute. I've got to go have a word with Mr. Hill."

"Ask him why Elliot knows my mama's word," I said.

Roy looked to Ruby for an explanation.

"*Soof*," she said. "You know how I told you Elliot says that a lot? Well, Heidi says her mother does too."

"And he called me *soof* today when he saw me," I said.

"Elliot says *soof* a lot, Heidi. It probably doesn't mean anything," Ruby said.

"I think it does. I think everything means

something, even when you don't know what it is," I said.

Roy smiled at me.

"Why don't you two wait out in the car?" He handed Ruby the keys. "Put the heater on, Rube. She's shivering."

Ruby carried my suitcase this time and I carried my backpack and the jar of jelly beans out to the car, which was parked at the top of the driveway.

I got in the backseat and Ruby got in the front so she could start the engine and turn on the heater.

"Do you need me to come back there and sit with you?" she asked over the back of the seat.

I would have liked that, but I shook my head no.

"Do you have any brothers or sisters?" she asked me.

"No," I said. "Do you?"

"One sister. Jill. She lives in North Branch."

"You have kids?" I asked.

I thought I saw a shadow cross her face.

"Nope," she said. "No kids."

Neither of us said anything after that. The

car heated up quickly, and the combination of the warmth and the hum of the heater made me feel drowsy. I rested my head against the back of the seat, closed my eyes, and fell asleep. I didn't wake up until we pulled into the Franklins' driveway and Roy turned the engine off. Even though I was awake, I sat there with my eyes still closed.

"Should we wake her up, or do you want to try to carry her inside?" Ruby whispered.

"What do you mean, 'try'?" said Roy, pretending to be insulted. "She's just a slip of a thing."

Ruby laughed. She had a nice laugh. Musical, like the wind chimes Bernie and I made once from a kit she ordered through the mail.

I don't remember ever having been carried before that, though of course I know both Mama and Bernie must have carried me plenty when I was little. Roy picked me up out of the backseat and carried me into the house, and I don't think I breathed once the whole time, just clung tight to the jar of jelly beans, which clicked and clattered as they knocked against each other. The only other sound was the soft

soof, soof of his shoes as he carried me carefully
up the steps, across the porch, and into the
house. I was sorry when he put me down, sorry
to have to open my eyes. It felt so good to be
taken somewhere by somebody, instead of having to get there on my own.

Roy and Ruby lived in a white house with
yellow shutters and window boxes all across the
front. There was a screened-in porch on the
side and a white rope hammock slung between
two trees in the yard.

Ruby showed me the little back bedroom
where she said I could change out of my dirty
clothes. Before I did that, though, I asked Roy
what Thurman Hill had told him back at Hilltop.

"Nothing. He said he wouldn't talk to me
without his lawyer present, so I'll have to go
back up there tomorrow to see what's what," he
told me. "Now go get changed, so Rube can put
dinner on the table."

I'd been changing my underwear and socks
each day since I'd left Reno like Bernie had
told me to, but I'd been wearing the same jeans
and T-shirt and the red sweater ever since I left
home. What I really wanted was a hot bath, but

I was too shy to ask, and besides, I was starving. I shoved my dirty clothes into the corner of my suitcase and pulled on some clean ones. I tried to run a comb through my hair, but I hadn't combed it in so long, it was really tangled, so I left it. When I went back out to the living room, Roy was sitting on the couch reading the paper. Ruby came out of the kitchen drying her hands on her apron.

"If I'd known earlier you were coming, Heidi, I would have made something ahead of time. As it is, frozen potpies will have to do. I'll make up for it with breakfast tomorrow, though, I promise. Dinner in about five, you two," she said, and went back into the kitchen.

Roy looked at me and smiled.

"She's no slouch in the kitchen," he said.

"Did you ask Thurman Hill how come Elliot knows my mother's word?" I asked.

"The apple doesn't fall far from the tree, I guess." Roy laughed. "Bernadette teach you to get right to the point, did she?"

I shrugged.

"Did you ask him?" I said again.

"Tomorrow, Heidi," he said in a tone I knew—when Bernie used it, it meant not to ask again.

We ate at a round wooden table in the kitchen. There were place mats with pictures of horses on them, and the paper napkins had flowers printed around the edges and were folded into triangles under each fork. I sat between Roy and Ruby. The potpies were filled with turkey and vegetables, the thick buttery crusts oozing gravy from little tear-shaped slits cut through the top. There was salad and cottage cheese and little bowls of applesauce sprinkled with cinnamon sugar.

I was so hungry, there was hardly a second my mouth wasn't stuffed too full for me to talk. For dessert Ruby dished out three big bowls of strawberry ripple ice cream, but I only made it halfway through mine before I ran out of steam.

"You look bushed," Roy said.

"It's no wonder—she's been sleeping on a bus for the past three nights. I'll run you a bath, Heidi, and then you can go to bed," Ruby said.

"Can I call Bernadette first?" I asked. "I'll call collect."

"Of course," said Ruby. "You show her where, Roy."

Ruby went to run the bath and Roy took me into his den to use the phone. We only talked for a minute. I told Bernie that Ruby and Roy were being really nice to me and that I was going to take a bath and go to bed. She seemed relieved to hear it.

"I'm not going to worry about you tonight, Heidi-Ho," she said. "Sounds like you're in good hands."

Mama called for Bernie in the background.

"I'm coming, Precious," she called back. "Your poor mama's had a headache all day long today. The worst one ever."

"Kiss her for me," I said, adding, "and tell her that I love her, Bernie."

Since *love* was not one of the words that Mama said, it wasn't a word I used very often either. For some reason that night, though, maybe because of the longing Roy had stirred up when he'd carried me in from the car, I wanted Mama to know that I loved her.

"I'll tell her," Bernie promised.

When I came out of the den, Roy was waiting for me.

"You got something to sleep in, or do you need to borrow something? I've got a big old flannel shirt that might do, or Rube's probably got something frillier you could borrow if you want."

I told him I had something in my suitcase and started to go back to the little bedroom where I had changed earlier. Roy stopped me.

"Heidi, does the name DeMuth ring a bell at all?" he asked.

"DeMuth?" I said,

"Diane DeMuth. Ever hear that name?" he said.

"I don't think so. Who is she?" I asked.

"Doesn't matter," he said. "Ruby's been running those taps for a while now. You'd better run along now and get ready for your bath."

I went to my room and opened my suitcase, digging around until I found the nightgown I'd packed. I fished my toothbrush out of the pocket of my backpack and went down the hall to the bathroom.

Ruby had run the bath so hot, steam was floating up out of it, and she'd put in enough bubbles to make it foam up like whipped cream. I'd seen pictures of bubble baths in magazines, but I'd never actually had one. Once when I had chicken pox Bernie put oatmeal in the bathwater to help with the itching, but that was lumpy, not like the bubble bath at all. I spent a long time soaking, and when my fingers were completely pruned and the bubbles had died down to a thin soapy film, I got out and dried off. I brushed my teeth and put on my nightgown and tried to comb through my wet hair, but it was even more tangled now than it had been before. I gave up. At least it was clean.

Roy and Ruby weren't around when I came out, and I felt too shy to go looking for them or to call out their names, so I went back to the little bedroom and dug my notebook and pen out of my backpack. I carried them over to the wooden bed and lay down on top of the covers. Then I flipped through the pages until I found the "Things I Don't Know About Mama" list.

What is soof?

was all that it said. Below that I wrote:

Why does Elliot know Mama's word?

I was too tired to write more, so I closed the book and slipped it under the pillow. Then I pulled back the covers and slid down between the crisp, cool sheets. I turned off the light and was already halfway asleep when there was a soft knock on the door and a wedge of pale light unfolded into the room. Ruby stood in the doorway.

"Everything all right?" she asked.

"Mmm-hmm," I told her drowsily.

"Need anything? Drink of water? Another blanket?" she said.

What I wanted right then was for her to come and sit on the edge of the bed, to read to me or scratch my back or talk to me the way Bernie always did at bedtime. On the bus sleeping had just happened when it happened, sometimes in the daytime and sometimes at night. But there, lying in a real bed like that in a real room, I wanted to be tucked in.

"I'm fine," I said, and wondered if that counted as a lie.

"Good night then," Ruby said. "Sleep tight."

"Ruby?" I said as she started to pull the door closed.

"Yes, Heidi," she said.

"These sheets feel different from the ones at home. Stiffer."

"They're line dried," she said. "Out in back."

"They smell like . . . sky," I said.

"I would have never thought of putting it like that," Ruby said softly. "Good night, Heidi."

I fell asleep that night thinking about all the people I knew in the world. Mama and Bernie and everyone else from home, but now I also knew Georgia and Roy and Ruby and Elliot. Their faces began to jumble together in my head, tumbling like jelly beans down the smooth sides of a glass jar. Right before I drifted off, I turned over; and as my bare legs slid under the stiff sheets, I heard Elliot's voice calling to me. Sooooooooof.

Roy came in to say good night—I heard him but I was too far away by then to answer. I had followed the sound of Elliot's voice into the dream that lay waiting for me on the other side. It was about Thurman Hill's watch. He came into my room holding one hand out to me, the cold, white fingers closed tightly around something I couldn't see. His sleeve pulled up as he reached out, and I saw his bony wrist with the gold watch. The face of the watch was blue, but there were no numbers on it, just four letters: *S-O-O-F*—one letter each at twelve o'clock, three, six, and nine.

"Show me what's in your hand," I said.

He smiled and shook his head.

"You'll never know," he whispered back.

Then he turned into a huge white bird with pale sea-glass eyes and flew out of the window.

CHAPTER SEVENTEEN

Kiss

I slept late the next morning. It was almost nine o'clock when I finally woke up, and the first thing I thought about was Elliot. I wanted to show him the photographs. I went straight out to the kitchen without even getting dressed.

"Where's Roy?" I asked Ruby, who was standing at the sink washing dishes. "He didn't leave for Hilltop already, did he?"

"No, he's gone to Monticello this morning," she said. "He had some business with the county clerk. Did you sleep well?" she asked.

"Like a top," I answered automatically.

"That's an interesting expression," Ruby said. "Where'd that one come from?"

"I don't know—Bernie always says it," I said.

"I've heard of sleeping like a rock, or like a

baby, but never like a top," Ruby said.

"Is Roy going up to Hilltop after Monticello?" I asked.

"He'll call in a while. We can ask him then," she said. "Want some pancakes? There's blueberry syrup I made myself last summer."

I was hungry, and pancakes with blueberry syrup sounded delicious, but I wasn't going to be distracted from my plan.

"Are you going up to Hilltop this morning to work? Could I come with you? I want to show Elliot my photographs," I said. "I thought maybe he'd remember Mama if he saw her."

"I'm taking the day off today," Ruby told me. "Thought maybe we'd spend it together."

"Won't Elliot miss you?" I asked.

I liked Ruby, but I didn't want to spend the day there with her waiting for Roy. I needed to go back up to Hilltop. I needed to be there to make sure somebody asked Thurman Hill to explain why Elliot knew Mama's word.

"I haven't taken a personal day all year," Ruby said. "There are plenty of other people Elly likes. There's Sally. She sings, and her voice is much better than mine. And he's got physical therapy with Bruce today. He likes that, too."

"But I want to show him the photographs," I said again.

"Show *me* instead," she said. "I only got to see a few yesterday. It's amazing to see how the place has changed. And I'd like to see your mother again, and your grandmother, too."

"I don't know if she's my grandmother," I said. "Do you think Roy could stop here first and pick me up before he goes up there? Or could you take me, even if you're not going to work?"

"Heidi, I'm sorry, but for the moment, like it or not, you're stuck here with me," she said. "Even if I wanted to take you up there, I couldn't. We only have the one car, and Roy's got it."

"Can I walk?" I asked.

"Much too far to walk. It's almost ten miles. Why don't you go get the photos and I'll make you a plate of pancakes," Ruby said.

I was disappointed, but there wasn't anything I could do. I went back to the little bedroom to get dressed.

When I opened my suitcase, I was surprised

to find that it was empty. I looked around and found that everything in it had been taken out, washed, ironed, folded, and put neatly into the top drawer of a small bureau near the door. The socks were rolled into tight little balls, reminding me of armadillos Bernie and I had seen once in an animal book from the library. The shirts and underwear were stacked in tidy piles, all the edges lined up and facing in the same direction. Tucked in among the piles was a small, nubby brown ball. It smelled spicy, and when I looked at it up close, I saw that it was an orange, stuck full of cloves.

The jar of jelly beans and my backpack were sitting on a shelf under the window near the bed. I pulled the packet of photos out of my backpack and headed back to the kitchen, where Ruby was busy at the stove, flipping pancakes.

"Thank you for washing my clothes," I said. "They smell good, and I like the way you fold."

Ruby smiled.

"You know, that bed you slept in last night was mine when I was a little girl, Heidi," Ruby told me as she set a plate down on the table for me. "It used to be painted blue, and underneath the edge on the right side is where I parked my chewing gum at night."

"Is it still there?" I asked as I sat down and pulled the folded triangle of napkin out from under the fork at my place.

"If it is, it's a valuable antique by now." She laughed.

There was a pitcher of orange juice and little juice glasses with sea horses all around the edges. Ruby brought a cup of coffee over to the table and sat down across from me.

"This ought to help make up for the frozen potpies last night," she said. "I made the syrup this past summer, picked all the berries myself."

I pressed my fork sideways down into the stack of pancakes. Blueberry syrup spilled over the edges and raced out to the rim of the plate like a little blue river. I took a big bite, closed my eyes, and groaned out loud, it was so good.

Ruby watched me eat, and when I'd all but licked my plate clean, she reached over and tapped her finger on the yellow envelope of photos.

"Will you show me?" she asked.

I nodded and wiped my lips with the napkin. Then I opened the packet the way I had a million times before and began to hand the photos across the table to Ruby.

"This is the one you saw already, with everyone out on the porch under the sign," I said. "And this is the one of Mama and the woman in the red sweater who might be my grandmother."

Ruby took the photo from me.

"And this is the scrawny Santa Claus—" I stopped mid sentence. The Santa Claus with his arm around the shaggy-haired boy. The unpadded red suit, hanging loose and billowing around his tall, skinny frame, the sleeves so short that his bony wrists poked out. And his watch . . . *his watch*. No wonder I had dreamed about it the night before.

I knew now who the Santa was.

CHAPTER EIGHTEEN

Bad

Roy called at ten to tell Ruby he was on his way back from Monticello.

"There's news," I heard Ruby tell him. "Mr. Hill is in the photos, Roy. And Elliot, too. He saw those photos himself yesterday, and he still told Heidi her mother had never been there."

Thurman Hill had known my mother. There was no doubt about it now. He had been at the party with Mama and the woman in the red sweater. People lie, but pictures don't. Elliot had been there too. He was the boy with the shaggy brown hair. I knew there was something familiar about him when I first saw him asleep in the chair, but with his hair shaved off, I hadn't recognized him from the pictures.

I had a hard time waiting for Roy to get

there. Ruby explained to him that I was very anxious to go back to Hilltop to see Elliot, and Roy had said we would talk about it when he got there. While we waited, Ruby and I went through the photographs again one by one, pulling out everything that showed Elliot or Thurman Hill or Mama. There were even a couple where all three of them were in the same shot.

"I just don't understand," Ruby said more than once. "He's a good man, Heidi. Why would he lie to you?"

"I don't know, but he did," I said. "He told me she was never there, and the whole time he knew she was."

"There must be some reason he's not telling the truth," Ruby said.

I thought about my list—

Sometimes people lie because the truth is too hard to admit

When Roy came back, the first thing he did was ask to see the photos. We showed him all the ones we'd pulled out.

"It's clearly him," Ruby said. "And Elliot. Look at his hair, Roy—it was curly. I'd have never guessed that."

Roy got a phone call, so I went to my room to get ready to go. I wanted to bring my notebook along in case there were new things to add to the lie list, and I also wanted to start a list of questions to ask Thurman Hill. I decided to wear the red sweater to Hilltop, so Thurman Hill couldn't lie about that too and say that it didn't really match the one in the pictures. I had just started to look for the sweater when I heard a car start up in front of the house and gravel crunch in the driveway. I ran out into the living room in time to look out the window and see Roy pulling out.

"Where's he going?" I asked anxiously. "He's just turning around or something, right?"

"No. He's going up to Hilltop," she told me. "Mr. Hill called to say he's waiting there with his lawyer."

"But I wanted to go too," I said. "Roy knew I wanted to show Elliot the pictures."

"Roy has the pictures," Ruby said.

I was really upset.

"My pictures? He took my pictures?" I asked.

"Only the ones we pulled out," she said. "The others are still here."

"He shouldn't have done that. He shouldn't have taken my pictures without asking," I said. "And he shouldn't have left without me. He knew I wanted to go. He said I could."

"No, he didn't. He said we would talk about it," Ruby said.

"Well, we didn't talk about it. And now he's gone," I said.

"He thought it would be better this way, Heidi," Ruby said. "Better to let the grown-ups sort things out."

"Grown-ups are the ones who tell the biggest lies of all!" I cried.

"He promised to call," Ruby said.

I wasn't going to sit around waiting for the phone to ring. I had a right to be there when the truth about Mama finally came out. It was cold outside that day, and the wind was bending the trees in the yard like giant gray pipe cleaners. I ran to the little bedroom to get my red sweater. It was all I would have to keep me warm on the long walk to Hilltop.

I was pretty sure Ruby hadn't put the sweater in with the other clothes in the spicy top drawer, so I pulled open the second drawer from the top. It was filled with impossibly tiny clothes—little shirts and nighties trimmed with ribbons and printed with patterns of lambs and kittens and ducks, most of them still in the wrappers or with tags attached. I didn't hear Ruby come in.

"Those belong to the babies I lost," she told me. "There were three." She was leaning against the door watching me, and if Bernie had been there, I know she would have said that Ruby's eyes told the whole story. I quickly shut the drawer, but it was too late— the sorrow caught in between those soft layers of pastel cotton had escaped and hung in the air now like a cold damp mist. Everything slowed down as the mist swirled around the two of us standing there together in the little back bedroom.

"I'm sorry, Ruby. I didn't mean to open it," I said. "I was looking for my sweater."

"I washed it last night. It's drying on a rack out on the porch," she said. "I should probably empty that drawer out anyway."

I could tell that sorrowful mist I'd loosed had wrapped itself tight around Ruby. I wanted to tell her I was sorry she had lost those babies, sorry that I had made her remember. Instead, I offered her the only thing I could think of to give her right then.

"There were one thousand, five hundred twenty-seven in here when I started. But I ate a few yesterday, so I don't know the exact number anymore. You can have the rest, though," I said as I walked over and lifted the heavy glass jar of jelly beans off the shelf.

Ruby brushed the backs of her hands across her eyes and smiled sadly.

"That's very sweet," she said. "Where'd you'd get those, anyway?"

"I won them," I said. "With a lucky guess."

"I believe it," she said.

She sat down on the end of the bed, and I sat down next to her with the jar in my lap.

"One thousand, five hundred twenty-seven, huh?" she said.

"Originally," I said.

I tilted the jar to one side and watched the beans tumble down through the glass. Reds, greens, yellows, pinks pushing up against each other, then going their separate ways, making and breaking up patterns as they went. I tilted it the other way and watched them shift and tumble again. I was the one tilting the jar, but it wasn't like I had any control over what happened inside it; all I could do was watch.

"It's not fair," I said. "He was supposed to take me with him."

"I know. But life isn't fair sometimes, is it?" Ruby said.

The phone rang then, and Ruby went to answer it. When she came back, she had my red sweater with her.

"I think it's dry enough now. Here, put this on and go comb your hair. Roy is coming to pick you up and take you up to Hilltop."

CHAPTER NINETEEN

No

Even though it was cold out, I waited for Roy outside. Now that I knew he was taking me to Hilltop, I wasn't angry at him anymore. The morning paper was on the porch, rolled up next to the welcome mat. I took it out to the rope hammock so I could swing and read to help pass the time until he got there. I'd combed my hair like Ruby had told me to, though there were still a lot of big tangles hidden underneath.

I got in the hammock and opened the paper randomly to the science section, where an article caught my eye. It was about dinosaurs and how nobody really knows what color they were because you can't tell by looking at the bones.

Ruby came out on the porch and called to me.

"Heidi! Bernadette's on the phone!"

I ran inside.

"Bernie, I'm sorry I didn't call you this morning. I've been so busy," I said. "I was planning to call you later."

"It's okay, baby," she said. "The reason I'm calling is because we need to talk about something important."

She sounded serious.

"What is it?" I asked.

"You need to come home now," she said. "Your mama and I need you to come home."

Going back to Reno was about the last thing on my mind at that moment. Any minute now Roy would be there to take me to Hilltop. I was sure he'd found out something important. Otherwise why would he be coming to get me?

"I can't come home, Bernie, not yet. I've got to stay here until I find out everything. Elliot says Mama's word, Bernie, did I tell you that already? And the Santa Claus is Thurman Hill. Roy's coming to get me right now. Something big is happening, Bernie. I just know it."

"You need to come home, Heidi,"

Bernadette said again. "Right away."

That's when I looked out the window and saw Roy's car pull into the driveway.

"He's here, Bernie. Roy is here and I have to go. I'll call you later and tell you everything," I said. I didn't ask her to kiss Mama for me, or even wait to hear her say good-bye. I hung up, waved to Ruby, and ran out to meet Roy.

"Whatcha got there?" he asked as I hopped into the front seat and closed the door.

I still had the newspaper in my hand. I must have taken it in with me when Ruby called me in to answer the phone.

"I was reading something about dinosaurs," I said.

"What about them?" Roy said.

"It turns out nobody knows what color they were," I said.

"I thought they were green," he said.

"That's what everybody thinks, but nobody knows for sure 'cause you can't tell from the bones," I said. "Did you show my pictures to that lawyer?"

"No," said Roy, "I didn't."

"Why not?" I asked, turning in my seat to look at him. "That's the only proof we've got that Mama was at Hilltop."

"It's complicated," said Roy.

"What's complicated?" I asked.

"The whole thing, but I don't want to talk about it until we get there," Roy said.

"Why not? Why can't you just tell me what you know?" I asked.

"It's really not mine to tell, Heidi. We're almost there—just leave it at that for now, okay?" he said.

I didn't understand, but I could tell Roy wasn't going to budge. We drove in silence for a while. Roy turned the radio on, and I looked out the window at nothing in particular.

It was Roy who finally broke the silence. As we turned off the road and started up the steep driveway to Hilltop, he asked me if I thought it mattered.

"If what matters?" I said.

"What color dinosaurs were," he said.

"Not really," I told him. "No matter what color they were, they're still extinct, right?"

"Good point," said Roy.

"But that doesn't mean I wouldn't still like to know," I said. "Wouldn't you?"

"Sure, but it doesn't sound like we ever will," Roy said.

"If somebody wants to know badly enough, they'll find a way to figure it out," I said.

"You think?" said Roy.

Believe me, Heidi, there are some things in life a person just can't know.

"Yeah," I said, not quite ready yet to believe.

Roy turned off the engine and reached into the backseat for his hat. We both opened our doors. As he put on his hat and got out of the car, he tilted his head back and looked up at the sky and I did the same. The sun was bright overhead and there was not a cloud in sight. A flock of dark birds was moving across the wide expanse of blue sky. Small parts of a bigger whole. I wondered if they knew that every time they changed the tilt of their wings, slowed down, or sped up, it altered the shape of the entire formation.

We walked up the steps past the rocking chairs and the pots of flowers, but right before we went inside, Roy stopped and put a hand on my shoulder.

"Heidi," he said, "some of what we talk about in here today may not be easy for you to hear."

"The only part that's hard is not knowing," I said. "I don't care what anybody says, as long as it's finally the truth."

"Shall we start with Diane DeMuth?" asked Mr. Dietz.

Thurman Hill's lawyer was short and bald and had a voice that sounded like someone was squeezing his neck whenever he tried to talk.

We were in the alcove. Thurman Hill was sitting in the red chair, where I had first come upon Elliot sleeping. It was turned around now, away from the window, and someone had brought in three wooden folding chairs for the rest of us to sit on. Mr. Dietz pulled a long white envelope out of his pocket, opened it, and took out several folded sheets of paper.

"According to county records, she was born here in Liberty," he said. "There's no record of a marriage, only a birth. A female child,

Sophia Lynne DeMuth, born to Diane at Liberty West Hospital, thirty years ago on November the twenty-third. According to the medical records, the child was born with significant damage." He stopped talking then, folded the papers, and stuck them back in the envelope.

There was an uncomfortable silence. Roy shifted in his chair and cleared his throat.

"I don't understand," I said. "Who's Diane DeMuth and what does this have to do with Mama?"

"It's complicated," Roy said again.

Mr. Dietz nodded, turned to Thurman Hill, and asked, "How would you like to proceed, sir?"

He didn't answer right away. Instead he sat there staring at his hands, which were folded in his lap. Finally the silence was more than I could bear.

"You lied about my mother," I said. "She was here and you know it. Why don't you just tell the truth now?"

Thurman Hill looked up then. I thought he would be furious at me for accusing him of lying. I expected the sea-glass eyes to be flashing angrily at me the way they had the day before, but instead to my surprise I saw that they were filled with tears.

"This is wrong," he said. "I'd like to ask you two gentlemen to leave so that I can talk to the girl alone."

"I don't want to be alone with you," I said. "Roy, don't leave."

But Roy and Mr. Dietz both stood up.

"I don't want to be alone with him," I said again. "He thinks I'm somebody I'm not."

"No, Heidi," said Thurman Hill, looking directly at me now. "I know exactly who you are."

CHAPTER TWENTY

Uh-oh

"Diane DeMuth is your grandmother, Heidi. And her daughter, Sophia, is your mother," Thurman Hill began.

It had not even been twenty-four hours since I had stood in front of that same red chair, hearing Elliot say Mama's word. Now here I was again, frozen in time as I heard Mama's name for the first time. *Sophia.*

"When Diane came to me asking for help, I wish to God I had turned her away, sent her over to Roscoe or farther north to one of the state-run facilities in Syracuse. Instead I let her talk me into accepting Sophia as a charity case at Hilltop. She stayed here at no cost to her mother for a little over a year. She did well here. She was happy, and she had a best friend. Elliot. They were inseparable, Sophia and Elliot. And I was so happy for Elliot, who'd never really had friends, I was too foolish to see what was happening. When Diane came to me with the news that Sophia was pregnant, at first I didn't believe it. And when she accused Elliot of being the father, I thought it was impossible." He paused. "They were like children themselves," he said.

I hadn't been looking at him as he spoke. Instead I'd kept my eyes fixed on the plant sitting next to his chair, the one with the long pointy leaves and the perfect little dangling flowers. I reached over then and took one of the fragile blossoms between my fingers. It came off easily and fell apart, the wrinkled petals falling down onto the carpet like tiny white tears. It was real.

"The chances of Sophia and Elliot producing a normal child seemed slim at best," he went on. "I felt the right thing to do was to end the pregnancy. But Diane refused. She insisted that she could raise the baby herself. I didn't want anything to do with bringing another damaged child into the world, not after I'd seen the way Elliot suffered. Diane pleaded with me, and when that did no good, she threatened to go to the authorities. Hilltop's reputation would have been ruined. I would have lost everything."

Thurman Hill sat forward in his chair, and as he moved, the sunlight coming through the big window behind him caught in the crystal of his watch, making a tiny circle of light dance up the wall.

"And so we struck a bargain," he went on. "I gave Diane enough money to take Sophia away to have her baby, and I agreed to give her more money every month to cover their living expenses. She chose the place, Reno, and I opened an account there, arranging for Diane's rent and utility bills to be paid directly from that account, so that I could keep track of how the money was being spent. She wasn't to contact me, not when the baby was born, not ever. I wasn't to know anything about their lives from that point on. I paid a small fortune not to know."

Promises have been made and paid for.

"I knew that Elliot would miss his friend, but I thought that over time, like so many things, he would forget Sophia. If I had known how wrong I was about that, maybe I would have done things differently. Elliot was never the same after Sophia left. He cried a lot and banged his head at the slightest frustration. And as if that wasn't enough to fill me with guilt, for the past thirteen years at some point in the course of every single day, he has said your mother's name. He never forgot her. The biggest mistake I ever made was to think that Elliot's love wasn't deep because he had no words to express it."

For the first time since he'd begun talking, I looked at Thurman Hill, *my grandfather*. There were dark circles under his eyes, as though he hadn't slept well the night before, and he was rubbing his forehead with his fingertips. Our eyes met, and then I looked away. He sighed and sat back in the chair.

"For thirteen years Diane kept her end of the bargain, and while Elliot held on to his memories, I did my best to forget. Then out of the blue I began to get calls from someone in Nevada named Bernadette. I thought it was Diane—I was sure it was. And when you came, I figured she'd sent you here to try to squeeze more money out of me. But there isn't any more. There's only Hilltop, and when I go, Hilltop is all that Elliot will have left."

Thurman Hill stopped then and looked at me.

"Do you have any questions?" he asked.

All this truth, spilling out around me, crashing over me in giant waves, left me sitting in the middle of the flood with nothing to say. What questions did I have? Only one. The same one I had started with.

"What is *soof*?" I asked.

He smiled sadly.

"It was Elliot's nickname for your mother," he said. "He couldn't pronounce Sophia. Neither could your mother. She called herself—"

I knew.

"So be it," I said.

"So be it," he echoed. And the way he said it, it sounded like "Amen."

Thurman Hill asked Roy and Mr. Dietz to come back in then, to help fill in the last of the blanks.

All those years of no rent or electricity

bills were the result of a bank account in Reno that Thurman Hill had set up to pay out automatically.

"Where is my grandmother now?" I asked.

It was obvious from the way they looked at each other that they'd been expecting that question.

"I'm sorry, Heidi, but she's dead," he told me. "I had the folks in Monticello run a cross-reference with Reno, and they had a certificate on file out there."

The death certificate Roy had found for Diane DeMuth listed the cause of death as a traffic accident.

"She was hit by a bus," Roy told me.

"A *bus*?" I said.

"Pronounced dead on arrival at County General Hospital in Reno, Nevada."

"Was it February?" I asked.

"Yes, the nineteenth," Roy said.

February 19 was the day Bernadette had found Mama standing outside her door holding me in her arms.

In my head a silent movie played. Mama and her mother, Diane DeMuth, standing on the corner, waiting to cross the street. Something happens, Diane gets distracted and steps off the curb too early right as the giant blue-and-white bus rounds the corner. Mama's dress blows up and she tries to hold it down with one hand. Someone screams. When Mama looks up, Diane is lying in the street. People come out of nowhere gathering around to try to help her. The driver jumps out and pushes through the crowd, leaning over her, feeling for a pulse. In all the commotion nobody notices the panicked young woman with the wide-set blue eyes clutching her crying baby to her chest and hurrying down the street toward an empty apartment.

"Done, done, done, Heidi, shh."

But of course I was only guessing, because, as I was finally beginning to understand, there are some things in life a person just can't know.

At a quarter to two that afternoon I called Bernadette. She took a long time to answer, more than ten rings. At first I thought maybe she wasn't there, but then I realized that was impossible. Bernie was always there. Finally she did answer, but she sounded funny—far away. I thought we had a bad connection.

"Can you hear me, Bernie?" I said.

"Yes, I can hear you," she said. "I've been waiting for your call."

"I have so much to tell you," I said. "You won't believe it. Mama has a birthday, Bernie, and a mother and a name. Mama has a beautiful name."

"Not now, baby," Bernie said.

That wasn't at all what I expected to hear. Normally she would have started right in asking me questions, eager to hear what I'd found out. Instead she asked me if Ruby was there.

"Ruby?" I said. "No. I'm up at Hilltop, Bernie. Remember, I came with Roy."

"And Ruby's not there yet?" she asked.

"No. She took the day off, Bernie. She's at home," I said.

"We'll talk later then," she said. "You'll call me."

"Wait, Bernie," I said. "Don't hang up. I want to tell you about Mama."

"Not now, baby. You'll call me," she said, and then she hung up.

I stood there holding the phone for a while, not knowing what to think about what had just happened. Why didn't Bernie want to talk to me? Why did she sound so strange? Maybe Mama had kept her up all night or something. I walked through the parlor and out onto the front porch to get some air to clear my head. Everything was still spinning inside. I felt dizzy.

It was cold enough for me to see my breath that day out on the porch, and I remember someone was burning leaves nearby. I looked up to see if there were more birds, but the sky was completely empty. I heard a car coming up the driveway. It was a taxicab, and I was surprised to see that Ruby was in the backseat.

I stood up and watched her through the window as she paid the driver. She got out and slammed the door, but when I think back on it now, it's strange that I don't remember it making a sound. It was as if the world suddenly had the volume turned down. The wind gusted and blew a strand of hair across Ruby's face. It caught between her lips and she brushed it away, tucking it behind her ear.

She didn't say hello, she just walked quickly over to where I was standing and put her arms around me, and suddenly I knew. That sorrowful mist I'd loosed from the drawer hadn't come looking for Ruby at all. It had come looking for me. As it worked its icy fingers into me and wound itself around my heart, Ruby whispered softly:

"Poor thing. Poor, poor thing."

CHAPTER TWENTY-ONE

Ow

Even though my grandmother and my mother died almost thirteen years apart, it felt as if I had lost them both on the same day.

After Ruby hugged me, she took me inside. Bernie had called her and asked her to be there with me when I heard about Mama. She dialed the number for me, and I held the phone to my ear and listened.

"Your mama went in her sleep, baby. I thought she was just sleeping off that awful headache. The one I told you about that was so bad. But after a while when she didn't wake up, I went to check on her and she was . . ."

"Dead? Mama is dead?"

As soon as I said it, I couldn't stand being inside my own skin anymore. I wanted to turn myself inside out, shake the feelings off like fire ants. It was all my fault. I'd been so wrapped up in what was happening to me, I hadn't even asked about Mama that morning. Bernadette knew she was getting worse.

Your mama and I need you to come home.

But I hadn't listened.

Bernie tried to comfort me. She told me I couldn't have made it there in time to say good-bye anyway. Ruby held me and patted my back, and Roy wrapped his big, strong arms around us both like string around a package.

We drove back to the house, where Ruby ran me a bath and tucked me into bed even though it was still afternoon. She brought me soup, which I couldn't eat, and sat by me until finally I managed to fall asleep. It was dark out when I woke up, and the house was quiet. I lay there for a while, trying not to think, trying not to feel. I wished it would all go away. I closed my eyes and pulled the pillow over my head. Something cold and smooth touched my cheek, and I realized it was the notebook I'd put under the pillow the night before.

I sat up and turned on the light. How could I have thought it was so important? So important to know. None of it mattered. Knowing didn't change what was. One by one I ripped the pages out of the notebook, crumpling them and throwing them on the floor until there was nothing left between the worn red covers.

I turned the light out and lay back down on my side with my arms crossed tightly over my chest. Holding myself like that, I rocked. "Done, done, done," I whispered as the cold damp mist swirled around me in the dark. "Done, done, done, Heidi. Shh . . ."

CHAPTER TWENTY-TWO

Done

"Don't be late tonight, Roy. I'm making a pot roast," Ruby called from the porch.

"*Pot roast?* Be still my heart. You haven't made that in ages," Roy called back.

"Poor thing's nothing but skin and bones," Ruby said.

"Oh, the pot roast is for Heidi, huh? If it was just going to be me tonight, we'd be having Pop-Tarts in front of the TV," Roy said.

"I've never served you Pop-Tarts for dinner and you know it, Roy Franklin. Get out of here now before I change my mind about cooking for you at all."

Roy took off his hat, ducked his head, and got into the car. He turned the car around, and as he drove past me, he rolled down his window and called out—"You haven't lived until you've had Ruby's pot roast, Heidi."

They were trying to make it seem normal, but nothing was normal anymore. I was out in the hammock, where I'd taken to spending my days curled up in a quilt in my nightgown and a pair of thick wool socks. Ruby sometimes came out and sat beside me in a chair, but we didn't talk. I didn't have anything to say. Bernie called a lot, but I didn't feel like talking to her either. I knew she and Roy were trying to figure out what to do about Mama and the funeral, but I really didn't want to hear about that.

A little while later Ruby came out of the house carrying a stack of magazines in her arms. She pulled the chair up beside the hammock, but I turned my face away from her.

"I know you don't want to think about it, Heidi, but we have to talk about tomorrow. Roy's going down to Sullivan County Airport this afternoon, to pick up the casket. There are some important things we need to decide."

I loosened one foot from the tangle of quilt and hung it over the edge of the hammock so I could push off from the ground and swing.

"I was thinking maybe you'd like me to cut your hair," she said.

I hooked my foot around the leg of her chair to stop myself in mid swing.

"Why do you want to cut my hair?" I asked.

"I thought maybe you'd like to fix yourself up a little tomorrow before the service," she said.

"What service?" I asked.

"The pastor from the Methodist church is going to speak," she told me.

"What's he going to say? He didn't know Mama," I said.

"Someone has to say a few words, Heidi," she said.

Roy had told me that he and Bernie had talked and that she'd decided that it would be best for Mama to be buried in Liberty, where she'd been born and raised. They talked about burying her in Reno, too, next to her mother. Roy made some calls and found out Diane DeMuth was in a potter's field on the west side of town, but in the end Bernie thought Liberty would be better. They'd asked me what I thought, of course, but I told them that I didn't care.

"I want you to look at these magazines," Ruby said, "just to give you an idea. I'm pretty good at it. I cut Roy's hair and some of the neighbors', too."

She left the magazines on the chair and went inside. After a while I reached out and pulled them into my nest. On every cover was a different beautiful woman with red lips and shiny hair and teeth so white and square and perfect, they reminded me of Chicklets.

I couldn't believe how many different ways there were for a person to wear her hair. The pages were filled with words like *upswept* and *feathered* and *windblown*, and over and over again *natural*. Wouldn't the most natural thing be not to cut your hair at all? I wondered.

I gathered the quilt cocoon around me and went inside, through the house, and into the bathroom. I opened the medicine cabinet and found what I was looking for. A pair of silver nail scissors. Standing in front of the mirror, I began to cut the tangles out of my hair, carefully at first, and then with angry chopping motions that hurt and pulled so much that I began to cry for the first time since Mama had died.

Ruby heard me and came and took the scissors away. She held me while I cried, and when I was through, she pressed a cool washcloth against my face. Then she ran warm water in the sink and gently washed my hair. Afterward I followed her out to the kitchen, still wrapped in the quilt, and sat on the tall kitchen stool while she cut my hair.

She turned the radio on and hummed along with the music while she worked, turning my head from side to side, steering me by the chin to make sure it was even. When she was finished, she dried it with a hair dryer and a big round brush; then she blew on my face and neck to get rid of any little hairs that might be sticking to my skin.

"Do you want to see?" she asked me.

I pulled the quilt tighter around my shoulders and started to stand up. A shower of curls and tiny brown prickles fell through the air and onto the floor.

"Leave the quilt here, Heidi. It's covered with hair," Ruby said. "No sense dragging it through the house. I'll sweep up in here later."

Reluctantly I shed the quilt, and Ruby led

me back into the bathroom, where she stood behind me, fluffing my hair with her finger-tips while I looked at myself in the mirror. I wasn't me anymore. I was some other girl. Some girl with short brown curly hair. Some girl with a new haircut and no mama.

"What do you think?" said Ruby.

"I don't know," I said.

"That's okay," she told me. "You don't have to know."

CHAPTER TWENTY-THREE

So Be It

We buried Mama the next day in a small cemetery near an apple orchard, only a mile or so
from Hilltop. Roy and Ruby were there, and
Thurman Hill, too, though he stood apart
from us, over near the gate where we first came
in. I had spoken to Bernie on the phone the
night before and told her I didn't want the
pastor to speak at Mama's funeral.

"I think I should do it," I said.

Bernie tried to help me come up with the
right words to say.

"When people die, we usually talk about the
things we'll miss about that person," she said,
"or the worthwhile things they did while they
were alive."

"Who the person was?" I asked.

"Exactly," Bernie said. "Who the person was."

That night, after Bernie and I hung up, I took a square of paper from a pad next to the phone and made a list. I planned to read it out loud the next day at Mama's funeral.

"Did you remember to bring it?" I asked Ruby as we walked across the wet grass to where Mama's casket lay next to a pile of freshly dug brown earth.

"Yes, sweetie, I have it," she said, patting her pocketbook.

We stood there for a minute quietly, and then I unfolded the little square of paper I'd been holding in my hand since we'd left the house.

Who She Was

Sophia Lynne DeMuth
So B. It
Precious Bouquet
Mama
Soof

I had planned to read the list out loud and not say anything more than that. But when I looked at Mama's word written there at the bottom of the page, suddenly something turned inside me like a key. I looked over at Thurman Hill, standing quietly by the gate, his hands shoved deep into his pockets, his eyes cast downward.

"I always knew that Mama loved me," I began. "I just thought she didn't have a word for it. But I was wrong. All along she had a word for love—it was just different from the one everyone else was using. We all had names for Mama— Precious Bouquet, Sophia Lynne DeMuth, Mama—but she didn't call herself by any of those. She called herself So B. It, and it didn't matter that no one else ever called her that; it was still who she was. A long time ago, somebody else who loved Mama gave her another name, *Soof*. But when she said that word, she wasn't talking about herself. *Soof* wasn't Mama's name; *soof* was Mama's name for love."

Then it was time for Mama to be lowered into the ground. Ruby opened her pocketbook and handed me a small package wrapped in tissue. Bernie had sent it from Reno, and I had asked Ruby to carry it for me, to keep it safe.

Unwrapping the layers, I gently set Mama's white tea cup with the gold rim on top of the casket. Next to that I put the big box of Jujyfruits I'd bought at the gas station where I'd asked Roy to stop on the way. One end of it was opened, because I'd taken out all the green ones and thrown them away.

I closed my eyes and thought about Mama. About the way she had looked the last time I saw her. Leaning out the window with Bernadette, waving good-bye to me as I set off on my journey.

"Tea, Heidi?" I heard her voice say in my head.

"Yes, Mama. Tea," I answered.

Then I sat next to her on the couch one last time and tasted the sweet hot milky tea. I saw Mama's smile. I felt Mama's hand patting my knee. I looked into her pale, wide-set blue eyes.

"Back soon, Heidi?" she said. "Back soon?"

"Good-bye, Mama," I whispered.

That night I was sitting with Roy and Ruby in their living room, still wearing the same clothes I'd worn to the cemetery. Ruby had put out plates of leftover pot roast, but nobody seemed to be very hungry.

"I just can't get over that haircut," Roy said, looking at me. "She looks so much older, doesn't she, Rube?"

He'd said that same thing three times already, just while we'd been sitting there. I think we all knew there was something we needed to talk about.

"We were thinking maybe you might like to stay with us for a while," Ruby said. "You could enroll at the junior high school in town and live right here with us."

"Give you a chance to get to know Elliot . . . and your grandfather," said Roy.

"We could paint your room. Wallpaper it. Whatever you like," said Ruby.

I looked at them sitting there side by side on the couch and thought about the Memory game. I wished the rules could be different, that there could be more than one match for every card. But Ruby had been right—sometimes life just isn't fair.

A few days later we stopped at Hilltop on the way to the airport. I stood with Elliot in the rec room in front of the big stone fireplace so Ruby could take a picture of us to show to Bernie. He didn't call me *soof* this time. Maybe I didn't look like Mama anymore with my hair cut short. Thurman Hill stayed away until we were about to leave. Then he came over and handed me an envelope.

"This is everything from the files about your mother. I've included some photographs, too, from the year she was here with us, and also of the rest of the"—he hesitated over the next word—"family. I think you'll find you look a great deal like the late Mrs. Hill, especially now with your hair that way. She was a lovely woman, Elliot's mother." I could tell that it wasn't easy for him, talking to me like that. After all, he'd paid a small fortune not to have to know I even existed. Before I left, he said one more thing to me.

"I know this is probably impossible after all that's happened, but someday I would like to know you."

Later I was glad I hadn't said what had been right on the tip of my tongue: "There are some things in life a person just can't know."

•　•　•

　　A lot of things changed after Mama died. At first I was sad all the time, but Bernie told me to feel whatever I felt until I was done feeling it, and even though I still haven't gotten over it, after a while I was pretty much okay. Ruby and Roy had planted a seed in my head, and I enrolled in the local junior high school in Reno, where everyone knew me as Heidi DeMuth. Zander and I still hung out in the afternoons, and we took turns baby-sitting for the Chudacoff twins. Bernie quit drinking coffee, because she read somewhere that caffeine makes anxious people more anxious, and she also decided to try to learn how to cook.

　　Another thing that was different was that after I came back from Liberty, my lucky streak, at least when it came to gambling, disappeared for good. Bernadette flipped coins for me sometimes just to check, but I only guessed right about the same amount a normal person would.

　　I did go back to visit Liberty. The first time was the fall after Mama died, when we put the stone on her grave. It was made of pink marble with the list of Mama's names carved on it in script. That, and the one that we'd kept taped to the inside of the kitchen cabinet in the apartment in Reno, are the only lists that remain from that time in my life.

Ruby's belly was big as a basketball that fall. Her baby was born a few months later. A little girl they named Aurora at my suggestion.

"We'd given up hope of ever having a family," Roy told me when he called from the hospital the day she was born. "Ruby's convinced you passed that good luck of yours onto her, you know."

I hoped she was right.

I didn't see Elliot or my grandfather that first time I went back. Roy offered to drive me over to Hilltop, but I just wasn't ready. It would take some time.

A few days after I returned home, I was waiting in line at the Double D in Reno when I spotted a box of Jujyfruits in the candy rack and tossed it onto the counter. Later, back at the apartment, I took it into my room and sat there staring at the familiar yellow box with the picture of the colorful candies on the front. I thought about Mama and Bernie and me and the life we'd had before I went to Liberty.

Suddenly I noticed something I'd never seen before. The name of the company that makes Jujyfruits is written on the side in small black letters inside a red diamond. *Heide*. It's not spelled the same, ending with an *e* instead of an *i*, but even so I'm pretty sure it would sound the same if you said it out loud. *Heidi*.

I wondered if my grandmother Diane DeMuth used Jujyfruits to coax Mama to do things the way Bernadette and I used to. I wondered if maybe she saw that word on the side of the box the day I was born and thought what a nice name it would make for a little girl. I sat there wondering those things until I heard Bernie calling from the kitchen.

"Come here a second, will you, Heidi-Ho? I'm trying to follow this recipe Ruby sent for pot roast and I'm making a mess of things. I need you to look up the word *braise* for me in M.B.F."

I tossed the yellow box aside.

"Coming, Bernie!" I called.

And I walked across the room past all that was missing, through the door, and into the light that shone like a sweet wide smile over all that was actually there.

Mama's Words *

Heidi
So be it
Good
No
Blue
Soof
Out
Hot
Bad
Done
Shh
Uh-oh
Back soon
Hello
Dette
Tea
Go
Ow
More
Again
Pretty
Now
Kiss

* Note: Two of Mama's "words" are technically not single words—*back soon* and *so be it*—but Heidi counted them that way because Mama never used the individual words, *so*, *be*, *it*, *back*, or *soon* except in those particular phrases.

EXTRAS

So B. It

Part I: Introducing . . . Sarah Weeks!

IT'S ALWAYS HARD to know what to say when people ask me to tell them a little bit about myself. Of course there's the regular stuff to talk about, like where I was born and where I live now. Then there are the harder, more interesting things to get into, like how I write my books and what's the best thing about being an author. Oh, and of course there's the question everyone seems to want answered—do I have any pets?

So starting with the easy stuff—I was born in Ann Arbor, Michigan, back in the days when there was no color TV, milk came in glass bottles and was delivered by a milkman, Barbie dolls came in only two varieties—blonde and brunette, and girls had to wear dresses to school every day, even in the cold, harsh Michigan winters when the temperature often dipped below zero.

My dad was an English professor at the University of Michigan who loved words, and books, and telling funny stories. My mother stayed home with my brother and sister and me until we'd all three gone off to college, at which point she went back to work as a bookkeeper in a law office. After going to college in Massachusetts, where I studied composition, I moved to New York City, where I still live today.

My sons, Gabe and Nat, were both born in New York City and have gone to public elementary, middle, and high schools. Even though they live in one of the busiest cities in the world, they still do all the same kinds of things other kids do—play sports, hang out with friends, and eat pizza. The only difference is that they play sports in Central Park, hang out with friends on Broadway, and the pizza in New York is sold by the slice.

As for how I write my books and what the best thing is about being an author—I think I'll answer the second question first. The best thing about being an author is that I get to spend all day doing what I like best—writing.

From the time I was a little girl, the two things I enjoyed most were music and writing. I still feel that way. Sometimes when I'm working on a book I completely lose track of time and, when I finally stop writing, I look out the window and am amazed to find that it's dark outside. Other times, when I feel blocked and the ideas aren't coming, I do my housecleaning instead, or bake cookies or, okay, I admit it, veg out in front of the TV for a while until I feel like writing again.

I'm one of those writers who believes in the idea that it's best to write what you know. I love animals, and I know a fair amount about them, so a lot of my picture books are about animals and the environment. I love kids—the way they talk to each other and the things they think are funny, so my novels are about kids. *So B. It* is the first novel I've written in which the main character is a girl.

I really enjoyed writing the character of Heidi. She's a much more serious person than any of the characters in my other books. Not that Heidi doesn't have a sense of humor; I think she does, but she has important questions on her mind and I enjoyed helping her find her way to the answers. I also loved being able to put some of my own childhood memories into the story—like when Ruby cuts Heidi's hair. My mother used to cut my hair out in the kitchen. I remember sitting on a stool with a towel wrapped around my shoulders and how it tickled when she blew the hair off my neck. That's why I had Ruby do that to Heidi. People often ask me if I was like Heidi when I was her age. I guess I was in some ways. All of my characters have parts of me in them, but none of them are exactly like me because they each have their own story, and I have mine.

Describing how I write is not an easy thing to do. I'm not ever sure where the ideas come from. Sometimes they seem to pop into my head out of thin air, and other times I see something, or hear something, or read something, and that triggers a story idea. Once I have an idea, the story doesn't always come out right away. Sometimes it has to sit in my head for a long time, being turned over and over again until I understand it well enough to start putting it down on paper. I work at the computer, but I edit with a pencil. I print out whatever I've written one day, and start the next day by reading it over and making corrections. Lately, I've been trying a new way of working, which is just to start writing and not stop until I get to the end of the story. I'm not sure yet if I like this new method. Every book I write goes through many drafts. Some more than others. With each draft I get comments from my editor and then I rewrite and rewrite and rewrite until we both feel the book is as strong as it can possibly be. I don't love rewriting, but it's just one of those things you have to do if you want to be a good writer.

Besides writing, I like to bake and talk on the phone and poke around in antique stores and go to the movies, and watch little league games, and visit classrooms around the country talking to kids about my books. It's nice being able to write both picture books and novels because it means that I'm always shifting around, doing different things. One day I might be working on a rhyming book about a clothesline, the next day a song about a penguin, and the day after that a serious book about a girl who goes on a long journey in search of herself. Variety, that's what keeps life interesting.

Okay, okay, you've been very patient. I know what it is you really want to know so I won't keep you in suspense any longer. Yes, I have a pet. He's a small brown mouse named Bing. His hobbies are running in his exercise wheel, building nests out of torn-up magazines (he particularly likes the covers of *The New Yorker*) and making noise at night. His favorite foods are sunflower seeds and Cheerios, and he wants you to know that he would very much like to meet a girl mouse—the sooner the better.

Part II: An Interview

Read on to see Sarah Weeks's answers to questions about *So B. It*.

How is this book different from any other novel that you've written?

Probably the biggest difference is that the subject matter is more serious. The books in the Guy series deal with some important issues like divorce and friendship and blended families, but those books often rely on humor to help get the point across. *So B. It* has its funny moments, but there are also some very sad moments, and Heidi is a deeper, more emotional character than any other I've written. In the end I wouldn't say *So B. It* is a sad story, though; I think it's a very hopeful story.

Where did the idea for *So B. It* come from and why did you choose to make Mama's mysterious word *soof*?

The idea for *So B. It* didn't come in one big chunk the way some book ideas do. Instead it came in smaller pieces that eventually began to take on the shape of a story. One thing I remember thinking about as I began working on the book was this idea that people are like locks, and in order to find out what makes them who they are, you have to find the right key to unlock the mystery.

With Mama, I decided that key would be a word, *soof.* I chose the word because of the "oo" sound. I just liked the way it sounded. It reminded me of words like *moon* and *truth* and *soothe.* Just like Heidi, once I settled on the word, I began to hear it all around me. One time, I was getting off a bus, and as the doors closed behind me, I heard it—*soof.* I decided to use that idea in the book.

Heidi's neighbor Bernadette loves words. She has a very color-ful vocabulary, and when she can't find just the right word, she sometimes makes them up. Was there anyone in your life who taught you about words the way Bernie teaches Heidi?

Absolutely. My father was an English professor at the University of Michigan, and at home we had a big dictionary on a table in the living room, just like the one in *So B. It.* We all visited it often for mean-ings of words, and pronunciations and, in my case, for the correct spellings since I've never been very good at spelling! I loved to be read out loud to and I have very pleasant memories of sitting at the din-ner table as my father read a section of the news-paper to us or something that he was teaching in his class. He really loved books and words and he passed that on to my brother and sister and me. My mother read to me every night at bedtime and my parents took us to the library all the time when we were kids. It was easy writing about Bernie's love of the library and how she liked to smell the

EXTRAS

books when Heidi brought them home since she couldn't go to the library herself anymore. I remember loving the smell of the library books, too. Actually, I still do.

What made you decide to make one of the main themes of the book "What is truth?"

I think it's a very interesting question. It's one of those questions that seems like it would be easy to answer, but then when you try, you find out it's a lot more complicated than you thought! What one person thinks is true may seem completely false to someone with a different point of view. Heidi wants to know the truth about who she really is, but what she finds out along the way is that sometimes the truth is like dinosaur skin: nobody really knows for sure what color it was, so all we can do is guess.

What inspired you to write *So B. It*?

One summer day, driving around in the Catskill Mountains with my sons, Natty and Gabe, I saw an old abandoned house by the side of the road. There was something about that house that called to me. I went back later and took pictures of it, and looking at those pictures, especially the one of the front door with its tattered lace curtain in the dusty window, started a story unfolding in my head. Humor and rhymes and music have always come easily to me. So has boyspeak—the kind of language that Guy and Buzz use in the Guy books. But I knew from the get-go that the story unfolding in my head wasn't going to have any of those things. It was going to be something completely new. It was going to be about a girl named Heidi. She was going to be lucky. And she was going to go on a long journey and end up outside that door with the lacy curtain in the window, looking for something. Herself.

How long did it take you to write *So B. It*?

I spent four years writing the book. That's the longest I've ever spent writing anything. I did many, many drafts and I sometimes got so frustrated that I had to put it aside and work on something else until I was ready to try again. I have written a lot of picture books, and also a lot of songs, since I was a songwriter before I was an author. In the end I realized that although *So B. It* was much longer than either a song or a picture book text, it still needed to have the same shape, the same arc, the same three basic parts—beginning, middle, and end—and that helped me to finally be able to finish telling Heidi's story.

Part III: *So B. It* as Reader's Theater

This spring I was invited to be part of a Reader's Theater event at IRA, the International Reading Association convention, in San Antonio, Texas. Avi, Richard Peck, Pam Muñoz Ryan, and I all contributed pieces and the scripts were arranged by Avi and an executive editor named Justin Chanda. The four of us split up the parts, rehearsed for a day, and then presented each other's work for an audience of nearly 700 teachers. It was astonishing to experience the reaction of our audience. Pam Muñoz Ryan and I played the parts of Bernie and Heidi in this excerpt of *So B. It*, with Richard Peck and Avi taking turns doing the narrator's role. It was very moving to me, and because so many teachers asked me afterwards whether there was any way they could bring the piece into their classrooms, we decided to include it here.

Heidi: One thing I knew for a fact from the time I knew anything at all was that I didn't have a father. What I had was Mama and Bernadette, and as far as I was concerned, that was plenty.

Narrator #1: Bernadette started off being the next-door neighbor, but that didn't last for very long.

Heidi: My mother loved me in her own special

way, but she couldn't take care of me herself because of her bum brain. Bernie once explained it to me by comparing Mama to a broken machine.

Bernie: All the basic parts are there, Heidi, and from the outside she looks like she should work just fine, but inside there are lots of mysterious little pieces busted or bent or missing altogether, and without them her machine doesn't run quite right.

Narrator #2: And it never would.

Narrator #1: Bernadette understood about Mama. She knew how to talk to her and how to teach her things. The trick with Mama was to do things over and over the exact same way every single time until she got it.

Heidi: That's how Bernadette taught Mama how to use the electric can opener. Every day for weeks she brought over the cat food cans and opened them in front of Mama.

Bernie: Watch me, Precious. Lift up. Put the can under. Press down. Listen to the hum. Done.

Heidi: Pretty soon Mama was saying the words along with her. Well, not all of them, but she'd nod her head and say

Bernie: done

Heidi: when that part came. After a while Bernadette let Mama try it herself.

Narrator #2: At first she couldn't remember what to do, she got the order all mixed up, but Bernie kept working with her and talking softly to her, and finally one day Mama opened a can all by herself.

Narrator #1: Done.

Heidi: I don't know who was happier about it, Bernadette or Mama.

Narrator #1: After that, Mama opened cans all the time. Soup and cat food and tuna fish. Any kind of can.

Heidi: In fact, we had to keep them hidden up high, or over at Berna-dette's, because if Mama saw a can she opened it,

Narrator #2: whether you happened to need what was inside it right then or not.

Heidi: Bernie taught me everything I knew and she was a very good teacher. When she explained things, they shot into my brain like arrows. She could describe an Arctic blizzard or cross-pollina-tion, and suddenly I'd be leaning into the bite of a freezing wind or riding on a bumblebee's back right into the middle of a snapdragon.

Narrator #1: Nobody ran in Bernadette's world—

Narrator #2: They skittered or high-tailed it.

Narrator #1: They didn't whine, they puled and moaned.

Heidi: She knew a million words, and when she couldn't find one to fit, she'd make one up. Like when Mama got frustrated and started scrunching up her face and working her jaw, Bernadette would say—

Bernie: Your mama's cooking up a royal rimple, Heidi.

Heidi: A royal rimple sounds like some kind of fancy pudding to me, but Mama cooked them up on a pretty regular basis and, believe me, hers didn't come with whipped cream and a cherry on top. I loved my mother, and I know she loved me too, but if we hadn't had Bernadette, we'd have been in big trouble.

Narrator #2: Heidi didn't tell Bernie the morning she went down to the bus station to play the slots and get her ticket.

Heidi: She thought I'd gone to the library. It was the first time I'd ever lied to her. I didn't like the way it made me feel, dirty or something, so I was anxious to set it straight as soon as I got home. When I told her what I'd done and showed her the ticket, she was livid.

Bernie: I've poured my whole self into you, Heidi, like warm milk into a bucket. Why are you doing this now? Why can't you just let things be?

Heidi: Because things aren't the way they're supposed to be.

Bernie: How are they supposed to be?

Heidi: A person is supposed to know where they came from, Bernie.

Bernie: We've been over this already. It doesn't matter where you came from, it only matters that you're here.

Heidi: Maybe that's what matters to you, but I'm not like you, Bernie. I don't want to be like you and I don't want to be like Mama either.

Bernie: Are you trying to hurt me? Is that what this is all about?

Heidi: It has nothing to do with you, Bernie. It's about me, don't you get it? You think I'll forget about *soof* and Hilltop and all the rest of it, you want me to forget, but I won't. If I do, I'll end up like Mama—full of missing pieces.

Bernie: The pieces you're missing are not important ones, Heidi.

Heidi: Don't tell me what's important! You don't know. You don't know anything. You want me to be like you, but if you really loved me you'd want me to be normal.

Narrator #1: Bernie turned her face away as if she'd been slapped.

Bernie: I feel as though I don't even know you anymore.

Narrator #2: She burst into tears.

Heidi: I cried then too. Partly because I felt bad about hurting her feelings, but mostly because I realized that what she'd just said was true. She didn't really know me anymore. I wasn't sure I knew myself. I wanted to go to Liberty, I needed to go, but I was also afraid and I couldn't admit my fear to Bernie, she would've pounced on it like a cat on a yarn ball, unwinding my resolve until it had no shape.

Bernie: It's not safe, Heidi. You're too young to go by yourself.

EXTRAS

Heidi: I didn't tell her that it also wasn't legal. Why should I fuel her fire when I knew she'd find out soon enough anyway? (*to Bernie*) I have to go alone, you can't come with me and neither can Mama. There isn't any choice.

Bernie: Yes there is: Don't go. Wait until you're older. Listen to me, I'm not saying forget about it, I'm saying give it time. We can keep calling Hilltop. We can keep showing your mama the photographs. Maybe she'll remember something.

Heidi: You're just saying that to try to keep me here. You know Mama can't remember things, Bernie. I don't care what you say, I'm going.

Bernie: You may not go to Liberty and that is final, Heidi.

Heidi: You're not my mother. You can't tell me what to do. You're not even family. You're nobody. Nobody!

Narrator #1: Bernie snatched the ticket. She was so angry she didn't even look like herself anymore.

Bernie: Is this what you want, Heidi? Is this all that matters to you anymore?
Heidi: Yes.

Bernie: Fine. Then go. Just go.

Narrator #2: She threw the ticket on the floor, stomped across the kitchen and through the doorway into her apartment, slamming the door behind her.

Heidi: It's the only time I remember ever having seen that door closed.

Narrator #1: At dinnertime, Bernie finally came over and heated up a can of stew. She spooned it onto plates for Mama and me, but she took her own plate back to her place. This time she left the door ajar.

Heidi: I put Mama to bed alone for the first time in my life. Luckily she didn't give me a hard time. I even got her to shower and wash her hair, which was usually Bernie's department. Later, I took my bath and when I was lying in bed, Bernie came in and sat down on the very edge of the bed.

Bernie: You mustn't lie to me ever again, Heidi.

Heidi: I had to, Bernie, otherwise you would have tried to stop me from getting the ticket.

Bernie: We both know I can't stop you, don't we, Heidi-Ho?

Heidi: I was going to New York myself. I felt a strange hollow sensation in the pit of my stomach

EXTRAS

and my mouth tasted funny—metallic, like the water from the drinking fountain at the library. I swallowed hard and looked up at the clear blue sky. It was comforting to know that a piece of that very same sky would be hanging over Liberty when I finally got there.

Part IV: The Guy Series

I THINK THE THING I've enjoyed most about writing the "Guy" series—which includes *Regular Guy*, *Guy Time*, *My Guy* and *Guy Wire*—is coming up with the dialogue between the two main characters, Guy and Buzz. I pattern a lot of it after the way my two sons used to talk to each other and their friends when they were eleven or twelve years old. Just like Buzz and Guy, they had some great, weird nicknames for each other—"Buckets of Nat" is one that my older son, Gabe, still calls his little brother, Nathaniel.

I use a lot of cereal names in the insults Guy and Buzz hurl at each other, like, "Give me a break, you Cornflake." Or, "Don't be such a Coco Puff." When I'm out doing my grocery shopping, I like to walk down the cereal aisle and try out all the names. Some work, and some don't. For instance, any kind of flake is good, but Shredded Wheat just doesn't cut it.

In the first book in the series, *Regular Guy*, the parents are married. I was married, too, when I wrote that book. But a year later, when I got divorced, I decided to have Guy's parents divorce also. I wanted to write about some of the things our family was going through, and also to show that going through divorce doesn't mean that you have to lose your sense of humor. My son Natty, who was seven at the time, asked if Guy's parents

EXTRAS

were going to get back together. When I told him no, he said, "Good. There should be books out there for kids like me."

I have a particular fondness for the mom in the series, Lorraine Strang. She's like an exaggerated version of me. I would never have the nerve to wear some of the outfits she walks around in or cook some of the crazy dishes she comes up with, but I do own a glue gun and I'm not afraid to use it!

Disney is in the process of turning *My Guy*, the third book in the series, into a feature-length film. Nobody has ever made a movie out of one of my books before, so it will be interesting to see what they come up with.